RAVENFALL

ALSO BY KALYN JOSEPHSON

The Storm Crow
The Crow Rider

RAVENFALL

KALYN JOSEPHSON

DELACORTE PRESS

Text copyright © 2022 by Kalyn Josephson
Jacket art copyright © 2022 by Ramona Kaulitzki

All rights reserved. Published in the United States by Delacorte Press, an imprint of Random House Children's Books, a division of Penguin Random House LLC, New York.

Delacorte Press is a registered trademark and the colophon is a trademark of Penguin Random House LLC.

Visit us on the Web! rhcbooks.com

Educators and librarians, for a variety of teaching tools, visit us at RHTeachersLibrarians.com

Library of Congress Cataloging-in-Publication Data is available upon request.
ISBN 978-0-593-48358-9 (trade) — ISBN 978-0-593-48359-6 (lib. bdg.) — ISBN 978-0-593-48360-2 (ebook)

The text of this book is set in 11-point Requiem.
Interior design by Ken Crossland

Printed in the United States of America
10 9 8 7 6 5 4 3 2 1
First Edition

To my sister, Adriane,

who taught me to value my heart

CHAPTER I

Anna

Everything looks different in the dark.

By day, Ravenfall's ballroom is all sparkling stained glass and high, arching ceilings—the perfect place to sit and sketch for hours. By night, my family's inn becomes a minefield of laughing guests, friendly locals, and what I'm pretty sure is at least one werewolf over by the fruit punch, judging by the bite-sized pieces of raw steak he's digging into.

The crowd would be fine, if it didn't make not touching people impossible. Before I turned thirteen and got my psychometry powers—a fancy way of saying *Congrats! You get visions of death now*—I'd have been weaving through the crowd, chasing down our cat Max before he could prank a guest.

Now I'm hiding in a plant.

You'd think no one would wander over to a dark corner overhung with singing ivy—currently rustling out a tune of "Twinkle, Twinkle, Little Star" and trying to wrap its crimson vines around my ankle—yet I've had to dodge a wayward guest three times already.

Granted, Ravenfall's ballroom is full to bursting. It's mid-October and the countdown to Samhain and my family's biggest party of the year is well under way, even if half the people here don't even know that Samhain is the Celtic origins of Halloween, or that it's pronounced *Sa-Win*.

But in the town of Wick, Oregon, where magic is never far from your fingertips, Halloween is the biggest holiday of the year, and Ravenfall is the place to be. Our Samhain party at the end of October is the only time the house lets down its magical wards, letting in everyone from the local witches and mazzikim to the selkies that live in Hollowthorn Woods. Under glamour, of course. We like to give the out-of-towners something to talk about, not run screaming from.

The house went all out in celebration, decorating the two-story room's white stone ceiling with a swirling galaxy of pastel pink and blue and yellow. Glittering mist gathers in the corners and spirals down in ribbons.

When the ivy starts playing with my hair (a curly hair "no freaking way"), I escape along the wall behind the buffet, where the house is trying to foist a slice of pumpkin cake with tiny orange icing stars on a baffled guest. I wonder how long he'll spend looking for strings that aren't there. The local magical folk know not to bother—the house can control the inanimate objects inside it, so long as it's touched them before.

I'm halfway to my new hiding place behind the bar when I spot my twin sisters talking to Mr. and Mrs. Andrade beside the stairs to the second-floor balustrade. The couple runs the animal shelter in downtown Wick—you know, cats, dogs, the occasional pocket dragon for the more magically inclined. They're laughing and smiling, Kara no doubt using her mind-reading abilities, and Rose using her empathy to entertain them. Locals in the know often try and hide their thoughts from Kara or emotions from Rose and see if they can guess them.

Jealousy pangs through me. I want nothing more than to be out there doing readings for guests or entertaining locals, but unlike the rest of my family, my psychometry powers are useless. When I touch someone who's seen death, I get a vision of it through their eyes. And asking people, *Hey, remember that time that person died?* is not a fun party trick.

Mostly I've gotten used to the visions—blood and monsters come with the psychic family gig, especially in Wick—but sometimes I touch someone who's seen a really bad death and I can't get it out of my head for weeks. The nightmares keep me up, no matter how much lavender Gran slips under my pillow.

Which is why tonight I planned to stay firmly planted in the ivy corner, but my plans have a habit of unspooling like a ball of yarn in Max's paws.

The twins spot me and detach from the Andrades, joining me along the wall.

"Taking the easy way out again, Anna?" Kara asks, always looking to get under my skin.

"Are you frightened?" In contrast, Rose is all willowy-soft voice and gentle concern. Of course, with her power to sense emotions, she can literally just look at me and know the answer to her question.

Five years older than me, they're already tall, but in shimmering silver dresses and matching heels they're practically skyscrapers. They share a knowing look that makes me want to introduce their nice dresses to the singing ivy. They're as different as two fraternal twins can be, from their powers to their personalities, but they always know what the other is thinking. Of course, Kara cheats.

"You know I can't go out there," I grumble, shoving my hands into my dress pockets. Kara always says pockets on a dress are tacky—and a missed opportunity for a cute bag—but I never wear a dress without them. What if I found a handful of faerie dust by the wood? Am I supposed to carry a bag around *everywhere*?

"You doubt yourself too much." Rose absently twists a red curl around a finger. "Don't hide from your powers, Anna. Embrace them."

"Like we do." Kara nods at a passing man with a feral grin. "Take that guy for starters. He forgot to put on underwear tonight."

"Oh," Rose says softly. "He's embarrassed."

"And that woman's a banshee." Kara points across the room at a pale-faced woman following an elderly guest a little *too* closely. She gives me a sly look out of the corner of her eye. "Of course, if you're too scared . . ."

I glower at her. "I am not."

Kara tosses her hair over her shoulder. "I bet you can't last a minute out on the dance floor."

"Watch me!" And to prove it, I dart into the crowd.

Immediately, I swerve to avoid two dancing men in glittering vests, then duck under the arm of a woman making sloshing gestures with her pumpkin root beer as she talks. I make it to an open space in the middle and slow, looking for an escape. I proved my point; now I'm getting out of here before—

I gasp as a hand brushes mine. A chill shoots through me in a burst of power I'm still not used to. Everything turns hazy, and suddenly I'm reliving someone else's memory. Compared to other

4

visions my powers have given me, this one is strangely warped, as if looking up through muddy water.

I'm in someone's motel room. A man stands at my side, but I focus on the one tied to the chair before me. His pale face is covered in bruises, but his gray eyes are resolute. He's not giving me the information I need. At his feet lies the body of a white woman with bright red hair and empty green eyes staring up into nothing. She didn't answer my questions either.

The man next to me nudges me aside, and I step away, bowing. His voice is the rush of autumn leaves, the air faint with the scent of pine. I can't make out his words. He wraps his hand around the man's neck. A golden light buds beneath his palm, flowing from the captive's throat and up the veins in the man's arms.

Then the motel room door opens.

A boy no more than fourteen stands just inside the doorway, another older teenager behind him. The younger boy drops his keycard with a gasp. The last of the light leaves the victim, and he slumps forward, dead.

Then I'm on the kid, tackling him to the ground. We wrestle. I nick his shoulder with a knife as he throws me off. There's a terrible sound, and I roll over to see a knife in the other man's ribs. The older teen pulls another blade out and sends it flying into the man's shoulder as he flees through the window.

All at once, the cold recedes and I come back to myself at the party. I'm on the ground, breathing fast. Whoever I bumped into—whoever gave me that vision—is gone.

Rose and Kara help me to my feet with identical frowns.

"Something felt off about that man," Rose says wonderingly.

"I couldn't hear his thoughts." Kara absently brushes some glitter stars off my dress. "Anna?"

But I barely hear them. I can't get the look on the dead peoples' faces out of my head.

"Anna?" Kara says more softly, but I only shake my head and pull away, fleeing from the party.

My pencil flashes across the page, trying to capture the look on the dead man's face. I can never get the eyes right, the way they empty when someone dies, like a candle flame smothered by its own wax. I smudge his iris with my finger, making the color steelier, more ghostly.

"Still wrong," I mutter. "He doesn't need eyes, right? Who needs eyes?"

I toss the sketch pad past the cup of Earl Grey on the kitchen table. It goes sliding off the edge, but a chair shifts aside to catch it before it can hit the floor. I give the house a halfhearted thankyou wave before dropping my forehead onto the table. Usually drawing helps me deal with my visions, but there's something about this one that won't let go of me.

"It was terrible," I say to Nora. "Like the time Max caught that faerie trying to poison the garden level terrible."

The faerie had survived, but there's still a spot in the garden where nothing will grow from all the blood.

"You were three. How do you remember that?" My mother doesn't look up from the already spotless counters she's wiping down.

The wood practically sparkles in the gold-red sunlight, but the house has been in a bad mood all day after straightening up from last night's party, and nothing cheers it up more than clean countertops and a cup of Earl Grey. The house could do it itself, but it'd be kind of like massaging your own shoulders.

"I'm a sponge of death," I mutter into the table.

She sighs, looking tired, and I wonder if a migraine kept her up last night. "Did you see anyone's face, sponge?"

"No, the vision was weird and fuzzy." I scratch the edge of one of the many sets of initials carved into the tabletop until the house scoots it out of my reach. I nearly tumble out of my seat, and I glower at the nearest wall until the house grudgingly slides it back. It's not my fault the worn wood is scarred with knife marks.

Nora makes a sound of consideration. "That can happen when there's strong magic nearby."

"Whoever I bumped into didn't even care about them dying," I add with a shiver.

The man hadn't died quickly. Death isn't as they show it in the movies. Bullets don't always kill instantly, and they don't leave just enough time for last words. Death lingers, clinging like campfire smoke in your clothes, and all I want is to wash it out.

Nora stops cleaning, her big brown eyes settling on me. My older brother started the tradition of calling our mother by her first name. The twins and I picked it up from him, and now calling her *Mom* feels weird.

"I'm sorry, love," she says. "I know how much these visions weigh on you, but you'll get used to your powers in time. Just give them a chance."

Ever since my ability showed up a few months ago on my thirteenth birthday, my parents have been trying to convince me how special it is, but I don't see how. I can only tell people things they already know. What's the point? I can't read emotions like my sister Rose or sense auras and summon spirits like Aunt Elaine. Mine's the only power in the whole family that's useless.

I belong at the inn as much as a vampire belongs in the sun.

Nora rests a hand on her hip. "It's terrible what happened to those people, but that vision could be ten years old."

"Maybe I can help find who did it," I say. "Point the police in the right direction."

Nora frowns, and I wince. A lot of things bring out her serious face, but I've hit one of the biggest: talking about our powers to nonmagical folk. We don't go to extremes to hide our abilities—this is Wick after all—but even here regular people believe in magic the way some kids believe in Santa Claus: halfway and for fun. If ole St. Nick really popped down their chimney, they'd call the police, which is why all the magical residents do their best to keep the truth under wraps.

Most of the people who come to Ravenfall come for our psychic name and services, but seeing and believing aren't the same thing. A lot of guests leave sure it's all a hoax, and those with an open mind aren't looking to tell the world, unless they want to get the Squiggly Eye Treatment—you know, the thing where people squish their faces together and wiggle their eyebrows around when you say something weird like, *I was talking to my dead grandpa the other night.*

I get that a lot.

"You know we don't get involved like that, Anna," Nora says sternly. "If it gets back to us, people start asking questions we can't answer, and that hasn't ended well for our family in the past."

"But I want to know what happened," I argue. "I *need* to know."

The wall behind me lets out a loud creak, as if the house is shifting its weight.

"See? The house agrees." I jab a thumb at the wall. It really needs a new coat of periwinkle paint, but the house won't allow it. Rose says it's because it tickles.

"The house always agrees with you, honey. You're the only one who has any time for it."

The only reason I have more time is because no one visits Ravenfall for *my* powers. While Nora tells fortunes, the twins read people, and Aunt Elaine talks to spirits, I sweep the porch and chase the sprites out of the garden. All I want is for my powers to be useful, for me to belong.

It doesn't help that I've always known that I'll inherit the inn. Nora's never said it, but who else? My older brother is studying to be a physics professor at MIT, intent on proving his powers through science, and the twins already have college scholarships, which just leaves me.

Plain, useless me.

I spin the mug of Earl Grey in circles as I replay the scene from last night over and over again in my head, looking for anything I might have missed. Who did I bump into? Why had they killed those poor people?

Glass shatters.

I jump, nearly knocking the mug off the table. Nora stares blankly at me. Glass shards the color of dried blood lay before her in a perfect crescent shape.

I sigh. That'd been one of my favorite cups. It's not the first sacrificial victim of my family's powers, though, and it won't be the last. My uncle once set my favorite couch on fire, and Gran has a tendency to leave objects floating on the ceiling. Nora always goes zombie-eyed whenever she gets her visions, and anything she's holding on to gets a gravity-induced reality check.

I love magic, but sometimes living with a family of psychics can be a real drag.

Nora blinks rapidly as the vision releases her. "Oh dear."

"What did you see?"

"Blood," she replies grimly. "And a new guest."

9

A dustpan launches off the wall with a small broom, and she steps aside as the house sweeps up the glass.

"That's so vague," I groan. Sometimes Nora's visions are as clear as a scrying crystal, but other times they're just feelings or impressions. This one can mean anything. There's not much I like about my powers, but at least my visions are way more specific.

She gives a *What can you do?* shrug and picks up the now-full dustpan. "How about this: I'll look into what you saw so we can put your mind at ease. In the meantime, do me a favor and feed Max before the guest arrives. You know how he gets around blood."

"Feeding Max is Kara's job this week."

Nora draws a deep, deliberate breath. As if *I'm* the difficult one. "Your sister has multiple guest readings today. She doesn't have time for chores right now."

Right. Because the rest of my family can entertain guests and make money with their abilities, and I can't, so who better to do all the chores?

"I think I'll be Cinderella for Samhain this year," I say. "Or maybe a redheaded stepchild."

She doesn't laugh. "Come on, Anna. That isn't fair. Is it really such a big deal to feed Max?"

Arguing with Nora is like asking a river to move out of your way, and this is an argument we've had too many times already. Though I can't help hoping someday she'll say, *You're right, Anna. Today you can meet with guests and Kara will do all the chores.*

"Whatever."

Ignoring Nora's look of disproval, I leave through the side door onto the wide wraparound porch. The auburn wood is warm under my bare feet, the last bits of mist persisting in the late-afternoon light. The house lets out a long, settling sigh, all its mismatched architecture and uneven floors relaxing in the warm sun.

Someone's already begun putting up decorations for Samhain. A fall wreath of tiny white pumpkins, brown autumn leaves, and sunflowers hangs on the white kitchen door, and faerie lights wind along the wrought-iron deck railing. Gran says they're powered by real faerie dust. Crush one, and you'll be granted a wish, but only something small, such as finding a lost sock or summoning a lump of sugar for your tea.

It doesn't do chores, though—I've tried.

A few months ago, I wouldn't have thought twice about doing my chores. I love living at the inn; I even love working here with my family. But now that I have my powers, I want to do something more useful, to actually be a part of Ravenfall, not just another set of hands. But to do that, I have to somehow prove my powers can be useful.

Maybe I can help the boy who opened the motel room door. The fuzziness of the vision kept me from seeing his face, but if I can find out more about the people who died, maybe I can find the boy too. Then I can finally put my powers to use and help them, and Nora will see I can do more for the family than just chores.

A ball of light bobs past my head.

The wisp stops, bright as a glowing headlight, and circles around me once, before zipping off into Hollowthorn Woods.

I watch it go with a frown.

Ravenfall sits at a weak spot in the veil to the Otherworld, where spirits dwell. The veil grows thinner as the end of the month approaches, letting spirits and other creatures cross over into the human world, but I wouldn't have expected to see wisps for another week.

I'll have to ask Gran about it.

My hunt for Max takes much longer than I'd hoped. The house tries to help, the walls groaning in different spots to lead me to him. But Max enjoys aggravating the house, and by the time I get to where it's sent me, he's already gone.

Eventually I head to the kitchen for a raw steak. The meat is cold and slimy against my fingers, but I don't mind it.

"I'm taking your food outside, Max," I call.

An elderly couple stands just inside the doorway, blinking at me in alarm and clutching their suitcases.

"Don't worry," I reassure them. "Max only eats dead things."

The man draws up, looking horrified, and I realize too late that didn't actually sound as reassuring as it did in my head. Embarrassed, I skitter past them, trying not to overthink it. Seeing me walking down the hall with a bloody steak in my hand probably isn't the strangest thing they've seen in Wick, and I long ago stopped trying to make friends with the guests. Or anyone, for that matter.

Who needs friends when I have the house and Max?

"If you don't come get it, I'm going to eat it myself!" I step outside onto the porch.

Juices trickle down my hand. I hold the steak off to the side to keep it from getting on my clothes. My worn jeans are one stain away from mysteriously disappearing after a trip to the laundry, courtesy of Nora.

A black shape trots my way from the woods surrounding the house. Max is trying to make me think he's been outside the whole time, but I know better.

The rumble of an engine fills the air as a cab comes up the driveway, momentarily distracting me from Max. It pulls in to the roundabout and stops at the base of the steps. The driver smiles and waves, but I'm more interested in the unfamiliar boy in the back seat. Is this Nora's mysterious guest?

He climbs out, a small duffel bag in his hand.

The first thing I notice are his eyes. They're an impossibly bright gray.

The second thing I notice is the blood.

CHAPTER 2

Colin

The first thing I notice is the house.

It's huge. Mostly Gothic style, all pointed arches and stained-glass windows draped in ivy, but the rest is a random mix of Victorian turrets, craftsman columns, and medieval stonework—all the styles I recognize from flipping through housing magazines late at night when my family has already gone to bed.

I spent hours thinking about what it'd be like to live in one again, instead of moving dank motel to moldy apartment every few weeks, a consequence of being in witness protection for the last seven months.

The second thing I notice is the girl. She has olive-brown skin and big brown eyes and wears a two sizes too big fluffy sweater with a headstone on it that says BRB. She's holding a raw piece of meat and staring directly at me. A black cat balances its front paws against her leg, trying to reach the meat.

The weirdness of it all almost drives me right back into the cab, but it took two days and the last of Liam's cash to get here from Montana. I have to believe my brother sent me here for a reason.

Thinking of Liam sends my heart skittering, and I look around for him, hoping he's beat me here. He went after the two men we found in our motel room a few days ago, making me promise that if he hadn't returned by that evening, that I'd do what my parents always told us to do if we ever got separated: go to Ravenfall Inn.

My mind stalls on thoughts of my parents, of my mom's still body on the floor, my dad's chin tucked to his chest as though he were only sleeping.

For the last seven months, my family moved and moved and moved, staying a step ahead of the people who were after us, and not once did my parents ever tell me who they were or what they'd done. Now they never will.

I hope Liam is safe. I can't lose him too.

"You take care now," the driver calls before pulling away a little too quickly. I don't blame him. He didn't really buy my "traveling to my aunt's" story, and between that and the dried blood on my flannel shirt, he probably thinks I'm in trouble.

He's not wrong. I just have no idea why.

I don't even know why my parents always told us to meet at Ravenfall. I'd looked it up once. Their website had a picture of the inn and a gimmicky description that said it's run by a family of psychics. I'd known it was in Oregon, so I followed the bus routes to Portland, where I got a cab. Except Wick hadn't come up on the driver's GPS. I had to fish out the paper map my parents made me carry from my emergency bag to find it.

After hours of driving through woods—far more than seemed right considering the distance on the map—the town had suddenly sprung into view, as much a part of the forest as the autumn leaves and thigh-thick roots. Entering it had reminded me of standing outside before a lightning storm, when the air is charged and thick.

It's how I feel inside right now.

I hold my breath, trying to focus on the way it makes my throat burn instead of on the anger and sadness wrestling inside me. Liam never loses control of his emotions. He's unbreakable, and I've done everything I can to resemble him the last few months, to not be a burden on him and my exhausted parents.

I have to be like him now more than ever—it's the only way I'll ever get answers about who killed my parents.

When I turn back around, the girl's still staring at me, but the meat is on the ground and the cat's gnawing at it.

Is that . . . blood in her blond hair?

It's from the steak, I tell myself as I carry my bag up the steps. They're lined with bright orange and white pumpkins, the ivy-wrapped iron railings tucked full of cornstalks and yellow leaves. There's even a life-sized scarecrow by the front door, and I nearly miss a step when its arms rustle in movement.

The wind, I think, then mentally smack myself for feeling uneasy. Liam didn't spend the last seven months drilling me in hand-to-hand combat to be frightened by a scarecrow. I was supposed to be able to defend myself in case the people we were running from ever found us. But they did find us, and all I did was keep running.

"Hello," the girl says with a smile. It's the kind that takes over a person's eyes. Mom's had done that too.

"Hello." I shift my weight from one foot to the other. "Is this the, uh . . . Ravenfall Inn?"

"Sure is. I'm Anna."

"Colin. Nice to meet you." I hold out my hand. She stares at

16

it but doesn't take it. Feeling awkward, I lower it and shift my weight again. Her brown eyes have a strange intensity behind them, as though she knows more about me than I do. Maybe she does. What if she reads minds and knows exactly what I'm thinking? I cringe, then push the thought away.

There's no such thing as psychics.

Anna smiles again, unblinking, but now she's not staring at me so much as *through* me. The cat is definitely staring at me, though. This is getting weird.

Then the cat leaps at me.

"Ha!" Anna catches it in midair, twirling in a circle. "I knew you were going to do that!" she exclaims triumphantly at the cat, holding him out at arm's length. "You're getting predictable."

The cat droops in her hands, looking defeated. Because apparently cats can look defeated.

"Anna one, Max zero!" She sets Max down, where he returns grudgingly to his raw steak.

"Sorry about that. He gets way too into his practical jokes. And he has a thing about blood." She gestures at my shoulder. "You should let my gran look at that while you're here."

The cut stopped bleeding, but it still hurts. It's from the same men who killed my parents. Liam managed to seriously injure one of them, and I hope it slows them down enough for him to catch up. He won't let them get away with this.

"Right. I'll do that," I say a second before the rest of her words sink in. Cats don't play practical jokes.

She regards me with that look again, making me feel out of place in my own skin. "No, you won't."

She's right. I've dealt with enough injuries on my own before. Most of them came from my boxing lessons with Liam. We've stitched each other up more times than I can count since medical care got complicated in witness protection, but he insisted I needed to learn. He was right.

"Are you here for a room?" she asks.

I nod. "Are there any open?"

Her gaze flicks over my battered old bag, and my uncertainty rises again. What if they won't rent to a fourteen-year-old who's all alone? I can't afford to go anywhere else, and this is where I'm supposed to meet Liam. I try to think of what he would say—he always has a quick word and a smile to answer everything. People like him, listen to him.

I, on the other hand, just stand there awkwardly until she smiles again and says, "Sure are. Just you?"

"Yeah. Actually, has someone checked in under the name Liam Pierce?"

"No Liams or Pierces," she replies.

My stomach drops, but I rein in my disappointment and follow her into a huge room with high ceilings and stained-glass windows with designs of strange winged creatures. A wide center staircase that looks plucked straight from a fairy-tale ballroom looms ahead. With all the open space and natural light, the place feels alive, as if the paintings on the walls might suddenly move.

Then the door swings shut behind me.

"Oh, stop it," Anna chastises without looking.

"That wasn't me."

"I know. I wasn't talking to you."

I glance around, but we're alone except for a couple guests talking over by a bay window and Max, who waits for us by the stairs. He's small and pure black with mischievous green eyes.

As we near, he pretends to lunge at me again, and I falter. Anna smirks. "Don't worry. He's just messing with you."

"Messing with me?" I repeat. "He's a cat."

"And a darn convincing one too."

Maybe *she's* the one messing with me. Either way, I don't have the energy for this, so I stay quiet and follow her up the stairs. All I want is to collapse onto a bed and shut the world out until Liam gets here.

"Some quick rules for your stay." She throws up three fingers and lowers them as she speaks. "One, don't damage the house. It damages back. Two, never make a bargain with anything in Wick. Of any kind. Just don't, trust me. And three, if you get lost, call for Max."

She swings right at the top of the staircase. "Oh! And if the mirror on the third floor asks you a question, don't answer it." She pauses, her face falling. "Actually, just don't go to the third floor. It has a tendency to disappear."

Okay, she's definitely messing with me. Ask Max? Disappearing floors? Maybe this is some kind of gimmick they do to keep up the psychic rumors and attract guests. Whatever it is, I'm not in the mood.

"What happened to your shoulder?" she asks abruptly, leading me down a hall. "Pay attention, by the way. I don't actually want you getting lost at night with no one but Max to show you the way."

I glance down at the cat, who flicks his tail intently from side to side, then absentmindedly rub my shoulder. "I'd rather not confabulate about it."

She casts me a sidelong look, and I add, "It means discuss."

A smile tugs at the corner of her lips. "Okay. No confabuwhat-evering."

We take turn after turn, the inside of the house as strange and mismatched as the outside. Some hallways are narrow and bricked; others are tall and sweeping, with great sunlit bay windows and delicate wallpaper of bloodred vines and fairies. The place is one turn short of a maze.

"Why is the house so . . . different everywhere?" I ask as we pass a reading alcove draped in midnight red velvet fit for a vampire's mansion. An elderly person sits in it reading a book.

"My family has lived here a really long time," she says. "People just kept adding on. The house hates it."

"You say that like it's alive."

Anna slows to a stop. "It is."

We stare at each other, but I resist the urge to call her a liar. This is all probably part of her family's act. Get people off guard. Gather info about them. Then use it all to make reasonable deductions about the guests so they can pretend they're psychic. I'd seen people do the same thing in the TV shows I used to watch before my life became an endless carousel of motels.

She wrinkles her nose and gestures to the last door in the hall. "That's your room."

"Don't I need a key?"

"The house will lock it for you," she says pointedly.

I spend a second debating if I *really* want to respond, before I mutter a quick "Thank you" and slide past her, shutting the door before she can say anything more.

It must be a corner room, because two of the walls are full of stained-glass windows. They have the same strange designs:

horses with fish tails and ghostly seals, pointy-eared faeries and big black dogs.

That's not the weirdest thing, though. The bed's headboard is black wrought iron with *actual* candleholders for posts, complete with thick wax candles, already lit. Perched on the headboard is a dark metal raven, its head cocked to the side.

Trying not to let my imagination run wild, I set my bag on the bed and unzip it. I hadn't been able to take much with me when we left our home in California seven months ago, but I at least have a few changes of clothes and some trinkets I gathered as we traveled. Not for the first time, I think longingly of the book collection I had before my parents uprooted us; Liam and I used to build forts out of them.

Sitting down on the bed, I unzip the smaller emergency bag inside, trying to ignore the twinge in my shoulder. Inside is a toothbrush and toothpaste, some deodorant, cash, a couple snack bars, a traveler's size bottle of water, a prepaid cell phone, a mini first-aid kit, and a pocketknife.

I also included my worn dictionary that I found in our first motel room. I'm already in the *S*'s. It's not the most fun, but it keeps me occupied. Books aren't cheap—not to mention hard to cart around when you move every couple weeks—and computers even less so. My parents had an aversion to all things trackable: phones, laptops, you name it, and we couldn't afford much when Dad went from being a nurse to a part-time grocer, and Mom quit working at the auto shop.

Besides, I figured out pretty fast that the bigger the words you use, the older people think you are, which is convenient when you need to convince a motel clerk that there's nothing suspicious about you checking out in the middle of the night while your parents shove everything you own into the trunk of a car.

I grab the water bottle, and the bag's contents shift, revealing a square of leather. Setting the bottle down, I brush everything aside to uncover a worn leather-bound notebook imprinted with an Irish trinity knot. It's my parents', and I'm sure that it was in my mom's emergency bag, not mine.

I check the tag inside where we each wrote our names in our bags, and sure enough mine's there. Where did the notebook come from? I flip it open. The page is blank. Every page is blank, as they've always been. But for some reason my parents kept it close to them, and I woke up more than once to find one of them bent over it in the light of a lamp.

Tossing the journal into the bag, I pull my mother's necklace from my pocket. The same trinity knot made of silver dangles from the black rope, a tiny emerald in the center. I'd taken it from her bedside nightstand before leaving the motel.

That morning, Liam and I had answered a local ad for a dog walker, even though we were never supposed to go out alone. But our parents had looked so exhausted, and I'd wanted to do something to help, so I'd convinced Liam to go with me. At eighteen, he was already sneaking out at night, though I never told him I knew, never asked why he came home with bruises and raw knuckles.

When we got back, we found our dad tied to a chair with two men standing over him. Mom was on the ground.

They killed him the second we walked in.

Now we're running again, and I don't even know why, not really. It's just another question I'll never get the chance to ask them. They're gone, and all their plans, all their answers, are gone with them.

For one long, guilty moment, I let myself be upset about that. Their silence. Their secrets. If they'd told me the truth, I wouldn't be where I am now, sitting in an inn owned by supposed psychics. I wouldn't be thinking about how I'll never hear my father sing while folding laundry again or come outside to find my mom bent over the old Charger, grease streaks in her red hair.

In that moment, I imagine how it'd feel to scream until my throat goes hoarse.

Then I shove it deep down where it can't distract me. I need to be strong if I'm going to get answers. And I will get them, one way or another.

I just hope I don't have to do it alone. Where's Liam? Before he took off after the men, he promised he'd be here, and he never breaks his promises.

I zip the duffel bag closed and put my mom's necklace on. At least I can wait for Liam downstairs so that I know the second he's here.

Picking up my jacket, I open the door and walk outside—and straight into Anna.

My hand brushes hers and she trips backward. Before she hits the ground, a chair skids over from the nearby corner and catches her. I gape at it.

"The chair moved on its own," I say dumbly. "Anna?" But she doesn't respond. She's staring at the wall in a daze, her pupils nearly as wide as her irises.

"Anna, are you okay?" I ask nervously.

A moment later she blinks, big and wide like an owl, and says, "You're the boy from my vision."

CHAPTER 3

Anna

The vision still had that hazy edge to it, everyone's faces too blurred to make out, but I recognized the scene. Experiencing his parents' deaths through him is worse than whoever I saw it from before. I can still feel Colin's grief, and I have to remind myself that the pain isn't mine, that my parents are still alive.

What are the odds that I would run into both the killer and the kid from my vision in the span of two nights?

In this town? Zero.

Shaking my head to clear it, I push myself up in the chair. "Why did someone kill your parents?"

Colin pulls his jacket closer to his chest, as if afraid it might try and run away. He looks lost, and I realize how exhausted he is. Those circles under his eyes would make a raccoon proud.

I wince. I could have phrased my question better. Or, you know, not have stuck my nose in something that's none of my business for once. But it's too late now.

"I, uh, had a vision," I say carefully. Colin's the type of guest who thinks the whole psychic thing is a hoax. If I'm not careful, he might—

The air comes rushing out of Colin's lungs in a burst and he bolts past me.

"Hey!" I spring from the chair after him.

He doesn't slow down. At the end of the hallway, he turns the wrong way. I fall into step beside him. "Look, clearly you're here for a reason, and I'm guessing it has something to do with your parents."

He only goes faster. I nearly have to jog to keep up with his long strides.

"There's no such thing as coincidences in Wick, Colin," I press. He takes another turn. We're almost to the front of the house now, but still far from the stairs he's looking for.

"I know who killed them!"

He stops.

I stare at him, wishing I could pull the words back. They're not true. I couldn't see the person's face, so I don't really know who they are. But I can find out—if he'll let me. Together, Colin and I can find the killer, and then I can prove once and for all that my powers are good for something.

"Colin," I say more softly.

Slowly, he turns around. His bright eyes are wide, the jacket clutched to his chest. I don't want to push him, but I need to know.

"You came here for a reason," I repeat. "What is it?"

He takes a slow, shuddering breath. "How do you know about my parents?"

Questions I can work with. People who stay here always have questions.

"There are three kinds of people who stay here." I hold up a hand, counting down each finger. "Tourists who wouldn't see a trap if it bit them in the rear, people who stay too late at our parties, and people like you. The ones who are looking for answers."

"Are you going to give me some?" he asks.

I raise a single eyebrow, a habit I picked up from my aunt Elaine. I prefer to think I don't look as silly as she does when I do it. "I can try, but you have to tell me exactly what happened."

Colin's entire body tenses like a coiled spring. I don't blame him. He's lost his parents, and he's here alone. He looks one wrong word away from running again.

I need to be careful. If he leaves, I'll never figure out what happened. My only chance to put my powers to use will be gone, a killer will go free, and Colin might never know the truth.

"If we're going to find the answers you're looking for, you'll have to learn to accept weird things." I try for a reassuring smile. "It's the only way this works."

"The way *what* works?" His voice cracks. "I don't understand. I don't understand why my brother sent me here or how you know about my parents or any of it!"

I cringe. I've never been good at this serious stuff. Kara always says my mouth moves faster than my brain. It's the same reason my parents moved me out of school, the same reason even in Wick, a place known for weird, I'm too strange to hang out with anyone other than a cat and a house.

It doesn't help that I can't ever seem to say the right thing.

I fumble for the words. Surely I can at least explain this without making him hate me?

"My power is called psychometry," I say. "When I touch someone who's seen death, I see and feel it as they did. Last night, we had a party, and I bumped into someone and saw the exact same thing I just saw when I touched you, which means they were there that night. I didn't actually see their face, but I can help you figure out who it was."

"How is that possible?" he whispers.

I approach him as I would a flighty wisp. "I don't know. Magic has always been a part of my life. Sometimes I forget how it can seem to other people."

Not just magic, but death and monsters too. People come to Ravenfall from all over the world looking for answers, and half my parents' friends aren't even human. Wick is so steeped in magic, it's in the air and the trees, even if not everyone can feel it.

Normally I don't pay too much attention to how people react, instead letting the guests decide for themselves whether I'm being serious. It's been a long time since I actually wanted someone to believe me.

"This isn't a trick, Colin," I say. "Magic is real, and we can use it to find answers about your parents."

When all he does is stare at me, my hopes sink. I'm asking a lot: believing in magic, trusting strangers, talking about his parents. But helping people is what I want to do. It's why I love working at the inn so much.

I just need him to let me.

"You think you can help?" he asks tentatively. "I can't go to the cops. My brother made me swear. He said they wouldn't understand."

"He's right." My family tried it once when a vampire was on a hunting spree around Ravenfall. The cops bungled everything and called us crazy to boot. "There was something strange about my vision when I bumped into that person; it was distorted, which is why I didn't recognize you. That only happens when magic's involved, and that's my family's specialty."

Colin studies me like a spectator looking for a magician's trick, and I turn out my hands: nothing up my sleeves.

"Okay," he says, finally lowering his jacket. "How do we start?"

Relief sweeps through me and I grin. "First, we get your stuff back to your room." I hold out my hands, and he uncertainly places his jacket in them. Plucking open a nearby laundry chute, I toss it in to the sound of his yelp.

"Don't worry! The house will return it to your room."

"The *house*?"

"Step one!" I throw up a finger. "Embrace the weird."

Colin runs a hand roughly through his hair, looking as though he already regrets his decision. Then his stomach rumbles loudly enough for us to both hear. His ears turn red as he asks, "I don't suppose step two could be dinner?"

Max is waiting for us at the top of the staircase. He springs to all fours, tail pointed tall, and trots over to Colin, weaving between his feet as I finish giving him Ravenfall's pitch.

Colin eyes him suspiciously. "So, let me get this straight. The cat is not a cat, the house is alive, and everyone in your family really is psychic?"

"That's right." I lean down to scoop Max up. "He's a Jabberwocky. They're guardians of the Shield between our world and the Otherworld, and they help spirits cross over."

Colin peers closer at Max, who promptly bops him on the

nose with a paw, startling him. I roll my eyes, plopping the cat back to the floor. "He's also a giant pain."

Max flicks me with his tail, impatient to get to dinner.

"Are all Jabberwockies cats?" Colin asks, absently rubbing his nose.

I snort. "If you ask Max, they should be. But no, they come in a lot of different forms."

"And the house?"

I lead the way down the steps and into the foyer. "The Hollow-thorn Woods outside the house is a super powerful source of magic because of how thin the Shield is here, and the original house was built from its trees. Even we don't really know more about its magic than that."

We join a thin trail of guests funneling down the hall toward the ballroom. A guest spots Max, remarking about how cute he is, and he raises his head proudly.

"And your family?" Colin asks. "Do they all . . . see death?"

I shake my head. "We all have different powers. Except my dad; he's normal. Well, sort of. He's a relic hunter. Those are mag-ical objects. He's on a hunt right now." Although my powers come from Nora's Irish line, my dad's Jewish side of the family has some magic of their own, though I haven't seen them in a long time. My last memory of them is when they came to the inn one October when I was really young, and we built a hut in the yard and ate challah dipped in honey. I remember we were celebrating some-thing, but when I asked my dad about it later, he didn't want to talk about it.

My dad doesn't talk about a lot of things, though. Like why he never takes his family's phone calls. Or why he goes on hunts for months at a time, leaving Nora to run the inn. But when he does return, he always brings me a new funny T-shirt and stays up all night telling me stories. I just wish he stayed a little longer.

I glance sidelong at Colin. With pale skin, dark hair, and shockingly bright eyes, he's the kind of cute Kara would have teased me about before I finally told her that I have no interest in romance and dating, and never will. The initial shock aside, he's taking all of this really well. I think he might even be starting to believe me. At the very least, he's willing to hear me out, and that's more than a lot of people would do.

Hopefully dinner will help him settle in even more, and then we can get started finding answers.

Colin slows, glancing at the front door.

"Who are you looking for?" I ask.

"My brother," he replies. "He's supposed to meet me here after . . . He went after the guys that . . . The ones from the room."

The ones who killed his parents.

"I'm sure he's fine," I say. "Wick can be a little hard to find sometimes. But the house will let us know if any new guests come during dinner." The nearest wall rumbles in agreement, and it's enough to snap Colin out of his trance as he stares at the wall in openmouthed wonder.

The sound of voices and the smell of food grow stronger as we enter the ballroom. People fill the round tables throughout, plates piled high with food from the buffet, courtesy of the house. Nora sits at our family's table near the far wall, which is more of a giant window. Tonight, the house has frosted it over, leaving little swaths of clear glass in the shape of pumpkins and falling leaves, and tiny crystalline lights bob through the room mimicking wisps.

I scoop up Max, flashing Colin a smile. "Remember what I said: embrace the weird."

CHAPTER 4

Colin

I've never seen so much food in one place.

My stomach grumbles at the anticipation of eating something other than frozen pizza or takeout. Before we started moving, my dad made a new recipe every night, and my mom always made dessert. I miss their cooking almost as much as I miss them.

The ballroom itself is no less impressive than the food. There's a small stage in the corner where three musicians pluck out a traditional Irish tune. Beside them is a bar, a huge wrought-iron raven with its wings spread mounted on the wall behind it. Its head swivels side to side, watching as a hundred different colored dispensers pour guests drinks of their own accord.

I dodge a woman with a foaming butterscotch-colored soda as I follow Anna. Like the grand staircase in the foyer, the dining hall reminds me of a ballroom from some long-ago castle, complete with dancing torches in iron holders along the walls. One of the flames leaps, taking shape in a flutter of autumn leaves, before diving back into place.

Anna grins at my astonishment. "They all think it's a light show." She nods at the guests.

I'm still gaping when we reach a long table, occupied by an older white woman who's nearly Anna's double, but without the faint smattering of freckles across the bridge of her nose.

"Colin, this is my mom, Nora Ballinkay," Anna says.

"Hello, Mrs. Ballinkay." I shake her hand, looking her straight in the eye and making sure to be extra polite. Polite kids get asked fewer questions, like *Why are you here alone?*

"Welcome to Ravenfall, Colin," she says with a smile. "You can call me Nora. Has anyone taken a look at your shoulder yet?"

My hand goes to the cut on reflex. That wasn't the question I'd been expecting, and I fumble for a response, but Anna cuts in, saving me. "Colin's the boy from my vision."

Concern furrows Nora's brow, and as if sensing an oncoming lecture, Anna dumps Max onto the table and says to me, "Buffet's this way!" before diving into the crowd.

We return from the buffet a few minutes later, me with two full plates and a rumbling stomach. Anna makes a mountain out of her food, then proceeds to make the weirdest mixture I've ever seen. She cuts her tri tip into tiny squares—Max snatching a piece here and there with an expert claw—and then mixes her corn and mashed potatoes together.

"I know you guys are psychics and not witches, but isn't a black cat kind of cliché?" I ask when Max bats a fork off the table.

"I tried telling him that, but he wouldn't listen," she replies, scooping the corn mashed potatoes onto a biscuit. "He's very stubborn. It runs in the family."

I don't question her, trying to do as she said and "embrace the weird." So far, the weird includes a sentient house, a cat that pulls practical jokes, and a girl who can see death. What could possibly be next?

Nora suddenly presses a hand to her head, her face scrunching up in pain. Then it passes, and she lets out a sigh. "It's about time."

Before I can ask what she means, the crowd splits and a tall, curvy woman emerges.

"Aunt Elaine!" Anna leaps to her feet, throwing herself at the woman.

"Anna!" She catches Anna in a big bear hug. Her black hair is piled atop her head, and tattoos cover every inch of her pale arms. There's something warm about her presence, the kind of person who just settles a room.

"You were supposed to be here at the start of the month," Nora says as Elaine releases Anna.

"So I'm running a bit behind," Elaine says breezily. "The weather was too good to pass up. Cold and rainy, just as I like it. Nothing beats Ireland in the fall."

Nora makes a noncommittal noise that sounds a lot like, "I wouldn't know."

Anna retakes her seat and leans toward me. "Aunt Elaine's son lives in Dublin, so she goes back and forth a lot. Nora's usually too busy with the inn to travel."

Elaine's green eyes fall on me, and she blinks in surprise. "Anna, how do you know Niall and Bridget's son?"

My fork clatters to my plate at the sound of my parents' names. I gape at her until Anna's voice snaps me out of my trance.

"You know, it's not polite to stare," she says, but she isn't talking to me—she's addressing her mother. Nora is looking at me so intently, it's as if she's trying to see my parents' faces in mine.

33

I try to wipe the ridiculous look off my face. "You knew my parents?" My heart feels as if it's detached from my chest, tumbling around in my stomach like loose change.

Elaine tucks some escaped strands of black hair into her messy bun. "Sure," she says in a gravelly voice. "Your mother grew up in Wick, and she and your father were regulars at Ravenfall. We spent a lot of time here together before they stopped coming about eighteen years or so ago. Wanted to quote, 'step back from the magical world,' wasn't it, Nora?"

Nora is still watching me. "Yes, because of the birth of their first son," she says tightly, and I get the feeling that's not the whole story.

I glance at Anna, but she looks as confused as I feel. Some small part of me takes comfort in knowing that she's out of the loop for once too.

Elaine settles into a chair across from me. "How are they doing, anyway? It's been a long time."

My voice sticks in my throat. Suddenly the sight of all the food on my plate makes me nauseous. For days, the truth of what happened has crouched in the back of my mind, an unrelenting presence. But as long as I kept it to myself, I could control it. To say it out loud . . .

The sound of the band and the chatter of the guests fades as if slipping underwater.

"They're dead," I whisper at last. "They were murdered a few days ago."

Elaine's lips form a very round O before she turns sharply to look at Nora. "You didn't know?"

"They were incredibly well warded!" Nora replies hotly. "I

didn't . . . I couldn't—" She sets her jaw. "They didn't want to be found, Elaine. Least of all by us."

Elaine drops her head into her hands. "Still, how could we not have known they were gone?"

"We haven't heard from them in eighteen years." Nora's voice warbles, and I realize that she's trying not to cry as much as I am. "There's nothing we could have done. Nothing they—" She stops, looking in my direction.

Elaine curses under her breath, the palms of her hands digging into her temples. "That was eighteen years ago, Nora. It shouldn't matter now."

Back and forth they go. I catch snippets, but I've begun to feel dizzy. Listening to them talk about my parents is too much. The room starts shrinking, the noise and smells pressing in. Anna tries to interject, but the adults don't respond.

I swear the room is spinning, everyone's voices growing louder and louder.

A piercing whistle cuts through the room. Everyone goes quiet, the adults and other guests all turning toward us with looks of surprise. Anna lowers her fingers from her mouth, and Elaine purses her lips. "I told Roy not to teach you how to do that," she says.

Anna ignores her. "Does someone want to tell us what's going on?"

Elaine looks away, suddenly very interested in a skull tattoo on her forearm.

After taking a deep breath to calm herself, Nora waves to the guests. "Nothing to worry about!" she tells them, before turning to me. "How exactly did you end up here?"

"My parents always told me to come here if we ever got

separated," I reply. "My brother went after the men who killed them. He's supposed to meet me here."

Nora frowns slightly at that, before nodding. "I'm sure he'll be here soon. Your room is yours for as long as you need it in the meantime."

"I don't have the cash—" I start, but she lifts a hand.

"You don't have to pay us. Your parents were very good friends of ours." She lays a reassuring hand on my shoulder. "You're safe here."

I start to say something else but stop as an overwhelming wave of exhaustion pours over me. I didn't realize how much I needed to hear that, even if the rest of their words have left my head spinning. What do they mean my parents wanted to step back from the magical life? And what did Liam's birth have to do with any of it?

Elaine stands. "I know just what you need."

I watch her disappear into the crowd, wishing I could be as confident about that. My parents rarely talked about their past, though Liam mentioned that they used to live in Oregon. Before we started moving, I went to school, ran track, hung out with my friends—normal things. If they were involved with anything magical, they hid it well.

Somehow, I'm not surprised to find another family secret. My life seems to be made of them.

"How did she know who I was?" I ask Anna, seeking an answer to cling to.

"Elaine can read auras and talk to spirits," she replies. "People in families have similar energy signatures, so she probably just recognized yours."

A pint glass of soda drops onto the table before me.

"Drink up!" Elaine claps me on the shoulder and retakes her seat, a mug of her own in hand. I study the drink, trying to decide if it's root beer or apple juice.

Anna leans over. "It's Wish Cider. It tastes like whatever you wish it would. We only give it to guests who know about magic. What flavor do you want?"

"Oatmeal butterscotch," I say doubtfully, and pick it up. The soda is creamy and smooth, the flavor identical to the oatmeal butterscotch muffins my mom used to make. But more than that, it tastes like comfort and happiness. It's all I can do not to chug the whole thing, to let it wash away the building emotion in my chest.

Anna holds her drink out to Elaine. "To the long and recently dead," she says gently.

"May they stay that way for the days to come," Elaine finishes solemnly. They hit the tops of their glasses together and then the bottom edge before drinking.

Eulogy, I think absently. *A speech or piece of writing that praises someone or something highly, typically someone who has just died.*

Then the words really settle, and a memory sparks to life. "I've heard that before," I say. "My parents used to say it."

"That makes sense, if they were a part of the magical community," Anna replies. "It's something we say to honor people who've passed, and to hope for a quiet Samhain."

She holds out her drink to me. "To your parents."

Something inside me seizes. My parents must have loved this house, full of music and people and food. They were comfortable in these kinds of places once, before they exorcised them from our lives. Moving so much the last few months was hard on me and Liam, but I know it wasn't easy for them either. Their lives changed too.

The knot in my chest loosens a little. I'll find the answers that I'm looking for, one way or another. But in the meantime, they would want me to enjoy this.

It takes me a moment to get my muscles working again, but I grab my drink and knock it against hers.

"To my parents," I agree.

That's when the screaming starts.

CHAPTER 5

Colin

I whirl toward the source, but Anna only sighs. "Here we go again."

"This is normal?" I ask.

"It's probably just Max messing with a guest," she replies, but then a second scream sounds, and a third. The house groans as if bending in the wind, and the lights flicker. Nora and Elaine leap to their feet, trying to calm the guests.

"Oh no." Anna's eyes widen, true panic flooding her face, and suddenly I know that whatever this is, it's not normal.

The ballroom descends into chaos. Guests sprint for the hall or the doors leading outside. I move instinctively in front of Anna, trying to find the threat. "What's happeni—" I stop as I realize what I'm looking at.

A man in a blue cardigan hovers two inches off the ground, half his body *inside the wall*. Another wears a black funeral suit, and there's a gaping hole in his chest. He walks straight through a guest as if he's nothing but a gust of wind. They're all outlined in a lustrous silver glow.

"Anna," I say as calmly as I can. "Are those people . . . dead?"

She gives me a strained grin. "More or less."

Definitely more.

"Max!" Nora calls.

The cat leaps from the table, landing soundlessly on the floor. His body ripples like heat distorting air. His shoulders broaden, his paws becoming bigger and longer as his entire body grows. Bulges extend from his back, his tail lengthening as spikes shoot out along it.

Then the little black cat is gone, and standing in its place is a huge creature, its body all lean muscle, with a square muzzle and a thick, angular head. Giant, dragonesque wings spread wide from his back, and jagged teeth protrude from his mouth.

"What in the world?" The question leaps free, and for a second, I wish I could do something *other* than ask questions. I feel about as useful right now as a wet blanket.

"Jabberwocky," Anna reminds me, before shooing me out of the way of a translucent man walking through our table. Now that Max is in the mix, her concern seems to have faded.

Max turns a nearly transparent ethereal silver and steps into the man's path. The spirit walks into him, and Max's body ripples, absorbing him like a drop of water into a pond.

Then he starts off around the room, gathering spirits.

I expect to be scared. When Anna started explaining her powers, it felt a lot like when you're in a car and the road dips, making your stomach swoop. Because as absurd as it all sounded, I believed her. The Wish Cider and ghosts flying about the house seal the deal, but rather than feeling nervous or scared, I feel curious.

"When this is over, you owe me so many answers," I say.

Anna gives me a strange look, a mix of pleasant surprise and excitement. Then her face pales.

I follow her line of sight over my shoulder and freeze.

My parents.

They stumble toward us, silvery and ghostly. My mom's normally laughing face is colorless and slack, and my dad's once-bright gray eyes are dull and empty. They both bear vicious purple handprints on their throats.

Anna tries to pull me away, but I don't budge. She tugs again. "Colin, don't look!"

But I can't tear my gaze away. My parents' heads loll unnaturally, and my stomach turns.

"They're dead." My voice splinters.

They stop in front of us. My hand moves on its own, trembling, as I try to touch my dad. My fingers go straight through him with a phantom chill.

His mouth opens and closes, but no sound comes out.

"What is it?" I swallow hard. "What did those people want? Why did they—" My voice catches.

"Why did they kill you?" Anna asks for me. My mom's attention snaps to her. "Why are you here?"

Their forms flicker like a faulty light. "Keep him safe," she whispers hoarsely. "They're coming."

Then they disappear.

All I can do is stare at where they used to be. Then Anna lays a hand on my arm, and I flinch, having nearly forgotten she was there.

"Are you okay?" she asks.

Shaking my head, I collapse into my chair and bury my face in my hands. But when I close my eyes, all I can see are my parents' empty faces.

"Colin," Anna says gently. I look at her from between my fingers. "Everything's going to be okay."

My gaze drops to her hand on my arm. "Why aren't you having a vision when you touch me?"

"I see only one," she replies.

Somehow, that little piece of information puts me back on solid ground, and I realize that's all I ever really wanted: answers. All the strange stuff I've learned isn't what overwhelmed me; it's all the questions that came from it.

I straighten, and Anna retracts her hand. The ghosts are gone, and Elaine and Nora move through the remaining guests, reassuring them. Max has returned to his feline form and sits licking one tiny paw.

"Did you enjoy the show?" Nora asks a young couple, clearly a rehearsed line. Just a performance, nothing to worry about she reassures them, and they seem to buy it. What else are they going to think, after all? That ghosts are real?

"What happened?" I ask. "My parents . . . How?"

Anna looks suddenly uncomfortable, as if she doesn't want to answer. "There are always spirits around in Wick. The closer to Samhain it gets, the easier it is for them to cross over. Every once in a while, one pops up and we pass it off as a projection, but even here, a flood of them is weird, and . . ."

"And what?" I press.

"Well, when people die violently, sometimes their spirits don't move on. Their unfinished business keeps them tethered to the human world."

My hands curl into fists in my lap. "My parents came to warn me. Does that mean I'm their unfinished business? That they won't move on until whatever this is, is over?"

"I don't know." She gives me an apologetic look. "First, I saw a wisp, which never happens this far from Samhain, and now this? It's not good, Colin. What's dead needs to stay dead."

Regret spills across her face when I flinch, and she plants a hand over her forehead. "I'm sorry, I didn't think—sorry. Come on. I'll show you back to your room."

I stay quiet all the way there, lost in thought as I replay the scene from the ballroom again and again in my head. It isn't until we reach my bedroom door that I realize the house never told us that another guest arrived.

"Liam—" I start, but Anna shakes her head.

"The house would have told us."

I look back the way we came, as if Liam might suddenly appear in the hall. What could be keeping him? If he'd found those men and had them arrested, he'd be here by now, wouldn't he? Unless he was still trying to track them down. Or unless— I stop the thought before it can form. Liam wouldn't have let himself get hurt. He wouldn't have left me here alone. He promised he'd be here.

I have to believe he will be, and until he gets here, it's up to me to find answers.

CHAPTER 6

Anna

Early the next morning, just after I've gotten out of the shower and finished getting dressed, there's a knock on my door. The sun's barely up, which is one of the big downsides of living at Ravenfall: the only time I get to sleep in is on Saturdays, which is our day off from chores other than occasionally helping a guest. Though with Aunt Elaine back to help and Uncle Roy soon to return from Ireland, I'll start getting Sundays off too.

My damp hair's soaking through my sweater when I open the door to find Colin standing outside in a pair of dark jeans and a black flannel shirt. Max sits beside him.

Colin had been extremely quiet last night. He went to bed without saying good night, and I half expected him to be upset with me this morning and not want to work together anymore. What he learned is a lot to take in, and I didn't exactly make it easier. Everything I said wrong is on replay in my head, and I make a vow not to mess up today.

Colin glances down at the cat. "I locked my door last night, but he was still on my pillow this morning."

"He's persistent."

"He's . . . a Jabberwocky?" He says the word uncertainly.

"You remembered." I grin. "Gran says they're super ancient, like the Shield, and might have even been created from it to guard the Shield and help maintain the balance between life and death. That's why Max helps spirits cross over. He's a kind of spirit himself!"

Colin's expression brightens. "You mentioned the Shield last night. What is it?"

Retreating into my room, I grab the towel off my desk chair and use it to squeeze the water out of my hair. "It's what separates our world from the Otherworld, where the spirits are. Ravenfall sits in a weak spot in the Shield, which is why we're a magical hot spot."

"It's like a rampart," he says. When I only look at him, he explains, "A rampart is the defensive wall of a castle." He gestures at the house. "This place kind of reminds me of one."

The house rumbles quietly in satisfaction.

Colin's gaze flits about my room, taking in the collection of incense holders (the dragon wrapped around the castle is my favorite) and movie posters for things I've never seen. The house hates electronics, and I don't have a lot of downtime for TV anyway, but I've always loved the posters. They make great art studies, and my attempts to re-create them are tacked up beside them.

For a moment, Colin looks sad, but before I can say anything, he asks, "Don't you have school or something? It's Friday."

"Homeschooled." I tried real school once in third grade, but

I only made it a month before the whole school was calling me Ghost Girl.

It's not my fault the cafeteria was haunted.

"So was I," he says. "Sort of. We lived in California until my parents were put in witness protection and we started moving around. They tried their best . . ." He trails off, his gaze growing distant. It's only been a few days since he lost his parents; I can't imagine how that feels.

"Witness protection?" I ask. "For what?"

"That's what I want to find out," he says. "I think it might be related to who killed them. And until my brother gets here, I don't want to just sit around. I want to find out as much as I can about those men."

Excitement buzzes through me, and I toss my towel over my desk chair, ignoring the house's rumble of discontent. "Okay, first things first, your mom's warning. She said *they're* coming, meaning more than one. I saw two people in my vision. Was that it besides you and your brother?"

Colin leans against the door frame, and Max winds around his legs. "Yeah, two men."

"Do you remember anything about them? Because I didn't get a good look."

"I . . ." He frowns. "I kind of remember the one that attacked me, but not the guy that . . . you know. But I swear I looked right at him. I can't remember his face, though."

"Weird." I frown. "The only thing I noticed is whoever's perspective I was seeing from bowed to the other guy. I think he works for him."

"He seemed really upset when Liam wounded him, so that makes sense," Colin replies. "The main thing I remember about him is that he was wearing a uniform of some sort with a logo here." He taps his chest.

I dig my sketchbook out from beneath my blankets and lean against the bed. "Can you describe it?"

"There was some sort of circle or loop on it." His eyes roll upward as he thinks. "The letters went through it. I remember it started with *Jo* and ended with a *C*." I sketch a loop resembling an innertube and then write *Jo* on one side and *C* on the other. "And there were thick specks all over it. Like rain."

I draw those, too, spreading them about like confetti, then turn the image around for him to see. His face brightens. "That's really good! I wish I could remember the rest of the letters."

"We can look it up online," I say, my face warming beneath his praise. "Once my hair dries, we can— What?"

He blinks at me. "Your hair?"

"Curly hair rule number one." I gesture at my head. "Never go anywhere with wet hair. Might as well invite the fuzz in and give it a cup of tea."

He grimaces. At least I think I'm funny.

"Fine," I say, slipping on a pair of brown fuzzy socks with pumpkins. "But only because Max likes you."

No sooner have I slid past him into the hall than Nora's voice echoes from downstairs. "Anna? Anna, these chores won't do themselves!"

I cringe. Apparently, Colin's arrival and an impromptu ghost gathering aren't enough of an excuse to skip my endless list of chores. I'm pretty sure Nora would keep on business as usual if the house flipped on its chimney and did a jig.

Max takes one look at me and bolts the other way. If he's anywhere near me, he'll be dragged into working too.

Tearing the logo page free, I hold it out to Colin. "You can use the computer in my dad's study if you want. I have to do some chores first."

Colin looks from me to the paper, clearly weighing something. "I'll help you," he says. "Then we can look together."

I fold the paper up and tuck it in my pocket before he can change his mind. "Come on!"

We start by locating Rose in the back garden, where she's sitting lengthwise across a pale wood bench wrapped in wrought iron, filling little cloth bags with various herbs. Her empathy has always been a little different, in that she's just as capable of reading the emotions of a flower or tree or even the house as she is a person, so she handles tending to the grounds. Which, if you ask me, is not a chore, seeing as she'd just do it for fun anyway.

She flutters a hand in greeting before we've entered her line of sight, and the hand stays poised over the air in front of Colin, shuffling side to side as if feeling along a wall.

"I agree," she says.

Colin blinks. "What?"

Rose picks up a pinch of bright purple petals. "My sister's confidence makes her very comforting to be around, though you wouldn't know by looking at her that she's actually a bundle of nerves, aren't you, Anna?"

My cheeks flush red. "We came for the pouches, Rose, not a reading."

"Anxiety is nothing to be ashamed of." She smiles faintly, tipping the pouches balanced in her lap into our outstretched hands. I quickly shuffle Colin away before Rose can say anything else embarrassing.

"Rose can read emotions," I tell him. "She usually understands you better than you understand yourself." Kara and I had made a game of guessing which guests would leave her readings in tears. There's something freeing about being understood so completely, and people return to see her a lot.

"What are these?" Colin holds up a sage-green pouch.

"Glamour charms," I reply, leading him inside and to the second floor. "We put them in guests' rooms so that if they encounter anything magical, the spell will make it so they see something totally normal. Unless *they're* magical—then they can see through it! Or if the magical thing wants to be seen, of course."

Together, we go through each room, knocking on doors and replacing the pouches in rooms where the guests have already gone out. We have to trek back to Rose for a second round, as the inn is already quickly filling with guests for Samhain. They mill about the garden, taking tea at the small tables throughout, and kids run through the hall, playing chase with Max.

A thin man corners us just inside the foyer on our way back in. "Young lady, there's a leak in my room."

"What did you do?" I ask.

"Excuse me?" He draws himself up.

"Whatever you did, apologize to the house. It's the only way it'll stop."

I brush past him, Colin casting a bewildered look in our wake. "What if he doesn't apologize?"

I shrug. "He must have hit a wall pretty hard to make the house that mad."

He's lucky the house didn't just drop him through the floor.

"Morning, Anna," calls Mr. Andrade when we knock on his

door. A short, Salvadoran man whose face falls easily into laugh lines, Mr. Andrade and his wife are regulars for Samhain, though they live just downtown in an apartment above the animal shelter they run together. Mr. Andrade is a psychic, and his wife is a shapeshifter from Ireland, and they prefer to be near the inn during the holiday.

"Sorry, Mr. Andrade," I say, holding up the glamour bag in explanation. "Forgot this was your room."

Mr. Andrade nods at the door across from his. "I'd do that room next. I heard them telling someone on the phone this morning that they had the most marvelous dream about a pure black horse with a mane of snakes." He smiles sheepishly. "I'm afraid my wife felt the need for a midnight gallop."

I salute him with the bag. "We'll take care of it."

Colin looks to me as the door closes behind us. "How can you possibly keep all this under wraps?"

"People are pretty careful about their magic, so these kinds of incidents don't happen a lot," I reply, knocking on the other door. When no one responds, the house lets me in. "And when people do see things, they usually explain it away themselves. It's easier than thinking ghosts and monsters are real."

Colin locates the bag where it's tucked in a flowerpot and replaces it. "I guess between that and these pouches, you don't get a lot of problems."

I shake my head. "If someone sees through the glamour and doesn't come up with an explanation themselves, usually they're very open to magic, and it's not a problem anyway."

We finish up the last of the pouches before sailing our way through several more chores. We give guests directions to town and help them choose restaurants and shops to visit, show them to reading rooms where my mother or Aunt Elaine awaits them, and help check people in. Colin helps me clean up spilled faerie dust on the deck, and we chase off a particularly grumpy gnome from the garden. Meanwhile, the house handles the simple stuff: cleaning, changing sheets, and delivering baggage.

As the last of the morning fog burns off, we head to the kitchen to help Nora carry food into the dining room for the brunch buffet we do on Fridays. Aunt Elaine, Rose, and Kara are there, too, since it takes all of us to get the food out. The house could do it itself but explaining floating platters of eggs and bacon is a little more difficult.

After inhaling our breakfasts, I grab Colin's hand and pull him down a side hall with me before Nora can corner us for more chores, releasing him as we enter my father's study. A warm, cozy room with a white stone hearth and curved walls that arch into a dome, the study is equal parts the dark wood paneling of a university library and the deep, cluttered shelves of a life-sized magpie.

"My dad's a relic hunter," I remind Colin as he takes it all in with open fascination. "He finds magical objects. Some of them he brings home, though a lot of these didn't turn out to be so magical. He's got a thing for tinkering, though."

I take a deep breath of the wood-scented air, the smell I associate with my dad, who hasn't been home in months. His trips take him around the world, and he's usually gone for long stretches of time, but it never gets any easier not having him here. Absently, I touch the writing on my shirt that says SHALOM IS WHERE THE HEART IS. It's one of the many he's brought me back over the years, and wearing them makes me feel closer to him.

I circle around to the desk, where my dad's computer sits. Colin peers into the reflective glass of a small mirror pinned between two gold posts etched with Hebrew letters, then at a metallic replica of a pocket dragon, down to the iridescent scales.

It winks at him.

"I don't even know how to begin searching for this," I say, pulling out the drawing I did and entering my dad's password (KUGEL, all caps). I try several searches in Google, starting by describing the pieces of the drawing, such as, "circle, specks, *Jo C*," but it just spits back random results.

Colin joins me. "Maybe we need to figure out what the circle and dots are first?" he suggests. "Try *Jo C* tire repair."

I do, and get an auto shop in downtown Wick, which I'm pretty sure is actually a front for a magical speakeasy with drinks that create illusions, if Kara is to be believed. Which honestly, she's really not. But their logo doesn't match the drawing at all.

"Jo C sprinklers?" he suggests.

On and on we go, trying every word we can think of to describe the dash marks and the loop, but nothing comes up to match the logo or name.

"I'm sorry, Colin," I say when he leans defeatedly against the desk. "We'll figure it out, but I have some other chores I have to do."

"Maybe a break will help," he says. "I might remember more of the logo."

We leave my father's office behind, joining the exodus of guests from the ballroom as brunch comes to a close.

"Are you still hungry after that?"

I look up at Mr. and Mrs. Andrade, both of whom are eyeing the drawing in my hand. When Colin and I only stare at them, Mrs. Andrade explains in her airy voice, "That's the JoDoCo symbol. Jo's Donut Company? They used to be a few doors down from the shelter, but they moved about a year ago."

Colin and I exchange looks, and a shiver trickles down my spine. This means one of the men who killed Colin's family was from Wick, which can't be a coincidence.

Something bigger is at play here.

CHAPTER 7

Anna

"Was JoDoCo a magical shop?" I ask the Andrades once my mind stops spinning.

Mr. Andrade shakes his head. "All human, as far as I'm aware."

They leave after we thank them, and Colin and I regroup at the base of the stairs. "What was a donut employee doing attacking people?" I ask.

Colin shrugs before inspiration lights his expression. "Now that we know their name, we can look up their business online. They might have a staff page."

I clap my hands together. "I can do you one better. My sister Kara is a computer whiz."

"Why didn't we just ask her from the beginning?" Colin asks as I slide past him up the stairs.

I hold up two fingers. "One, because even Kara can't make something out of nothing, and two, because it's Kara, and I'd rather ask a Grindylow for help."

"A what?"

"Water demon. Drowns kids who come too close to the water. Though really quite sweet if you feed them Hawthorne berries in the winter mont— What?"

Colin only sighs. "Your life is even stranger than mine."

I grin.

The twins' room is down the hall from mine, before a tall stained-glass window depicting the tree of life. Everyone in my family has a room in Ravenfall, but only the twins, Nora, and I are here full-time. My aunt and uncle go back and forth between Wick and Ireland, and Gran lives above her tea shop.

You'd *think* that'd mean I could have a little independence and move into a room far, far away from the twins', but the house wants to keep all our rooms close together and separate from the guests. It's one of the few ways it finds order in its messy halls.

The fast-paced beat of Irish music floats out from inside the room, and I enter without knocking. Kara already knows we're there anyway.

"Morning!" she calls without looking up from her computer.

Rose lies on her stomach upon a plush lavender throw rug, organizing pieces of sea glass. She waves.

Rose and Kara's room looks like someone split it in two and tried to pack an electronics store on one side and a greenhouse on the other. Kara's walls are lined with computers and monitors, different agendas flitting from screen to screen that she uses to handle day-to-day scheduling for the inn, from keeping track of open rooms to booking readings. Her desk is scattered with key-boards, wires, and flash drives, while Rose's is a step away from a planter box, filled to the edge with small pots of bright flowers and grids of herbs. Hanging pots take up most of the ceiling, filled with bundles of fennel and the gemstones our dad always brings her back from his trips.

I know Kara's absurd amount of electronics bothers the house to no end, but she refuses to do anything about it. She's eighteen now and her war with the house started the day she was born.

"Hi, Colin," Kara greets, setting down her pumpkin spice latte. I can smell the cinnamon from here. She gestures at the purple La-Z-Boy in the corner. "Have a seat. I agree—you definitely should have come to me from the beginning."

Colin glances at me, and I wince. "Kara can read minds. But only what's on the surface!" I add as he blanches.

"Like what you're thinking right now," Kara says, tossing her strawberry-blond hair over her shoulder. There are tiny glass ghost charms braided into it today. "About your parents. I've already pulled up JoDoCo's old website."

A couple clicks, and the huge monitor on the wall fills with the donut company's website, already open to the staff page.

I plop down on the lower bunk of their stacked beds. Rose offers me a strand of wire and a handful of glass, and I start threading the two together, the glass buzzing lightly against my fingers—Rose's girlfriend, Dilara, must have spelled it for something. These will probably go in the garden, where they'll repel kesilim or attract wisps.

"Anyone look familiar?" Kara scrolls through the web page and Colin moves closer, peering up at the screen.

"There, stop!" He points at a picture of a man named Kaden Richards. Kara zooms in on Kaden's photo, revealing a white man in his late thirties with half-lidded green eyes who looks like he's mid-yawn. He seems harmless.

"Is there anything there that might explain why he helped someone kill my parents?" Colin asks it steadily, but his hands are clenched into fists.

"Maybe." Kara's fingers tap across the keyboard with the speed of a hummingbird's wings.

Unlike Kara, I can barely operate a toaster, so her skill with computers never ceases to amaze me. Of course, her powers help. Computers and the internet are basically a collective mind, which makes getting around inside them a lot easier for a mind reader.

I feel a pang of jealousy at how good she is with her powers—Rose too. They always turn up something useful, and they make it look so easy. All I've done for Colin is accidentally remind him of his dead parents a few times and fail at using the internet.

I feel a reassuring pat on my leg from Rose and give her a weak smile.

Security camera footage pops up on the screen, showing Kaden's profile. But that's not what surprises me—it's where he is.

"He's downtown!" I toss the wire aside.

"What?" Colin says at the same time Kara says, "That's not all."

Kara pauses the video of Kaden, rewinds, and then zooms in on Kaden's face as he turns briefly to look in the direction of the camera.

His eyes are pure silver, the pupil gone.

I gasp. "I knew it! He's magical."

"What?" Colin repeats.

"Supernatural creatures' eyes turn silver on camera," Rose explains. "Whatever Kaden is, he's not human."

"I thought he might be since something made the vision all fuzzy," I say, though I hadn't been sure if it was Kaden, the man Liam wounded, or both. "What's he doing downtown?"

Rose hums quietly. "He's looking for something. I can feel his frustration."

With all psychic powers, some people's specific abilities are stronger than others, and Gran says Rose is one of the most powerful empaths she's ever met. She can feel almost all of Wick. It's why she's halfway distracted all the time—there's too much else to listen to.

"Colin, that's not a good idea," Kara says to some thought only she can hear.

Colin stares at her for a heartbeat, then drops his head. "Yeah, you're right. I just need a minute." He slips from the room.

"What?" I ask.

"He wanted to go after him," Kara explains with a roll of her eyes.

Leaping off the bed, I bolt from the room before my thoughts can settle enough for Kara to pick up on.

Max. Max. Max. Max. Max, I think over and over again.

"Anna, I know what you're doing!" Kara's voice follows me into the hall, but I keep repeating Max's name until I catch up with Colin. It's hard not to think about something you don't want Kara to hear, because by thinking about not thinking about it, you always end up thinking about it. So instead, I pick one thought and repeat it to muddle everything until I'm a safe distance away.

"Did you change your mind about going after Kaden?" I ask, already sure I know his answer.

"Nope," he says without stopping. "I just didn't want Kara to know."

I grin. This is our chance. If we can find Kaden, maybe he can lead us to the man Liam wounded. Then Colin can get some answers, and my family will see that for once, my powers are just as useful as everyone else's.

We stop by my room so I can put on a pair of rainboots. Max joins us, and then we're off again. Max bounds ahead down the stairs, then meets us at the base with a nod at the kitchen: the coast is clear. When I head straight for it, Colin hesitates.

"Where are you going?" He gestures at the front door.

"If Nora sees us, she won't let us go," I say, highly doubting she'd take "we're hunting a potentially evil magical creature" as a good excuse for shirking my chores. "Besides, we need a ride."

Halfway through the kitchen, I snag a slice of apple pie off the counter, then leap from the side deck and head for Hollowthorn Woods. The leaves rustle in greeting and I wave to the nearest oak. Colin follows, his face full of curiosity, until I stop before the big oak tree we call Grandpa. It's so big around it'd take my whole family holding hands to reach around it.

"Hello," I say to the tree. "Will you please take us to the Merrow?"

I set the pie down by its roots. Its favorite is strawberry rhubarb, but it's never been picky about pie, and it's always had a soft spot for Gran. I'm pretty sure it'd take us to her tea shop even if I didn't give it anything.

"Um, Anna," Colin says quietly. "You're talking to a tree."

"Embrace the weird," I sing back at him with a grin.

Then the tree unravels.

CHAPTER 8

Colin

The tree peels apart like a paper straw unwinding, revealing a dark alcove inside that smells of wet earth. The shock is enough to make my blood go still—until Max goes flying past me and vanishes into the dark.

I lurch after him, but Anna only laughs. "Oh no you don't!" she yells, leaping in too.

She disappears.

"Great," I say with a sigh. Either this is a magical portal, or I'm about to crash into a girl and a cat. Is this how Alice felt falling down the rabbit hole? I suppose that makes Max the White Rabbit. And Anna?

Definitely the Mad Hatter.

Taking a breath, I step into the tree.

The strangest sensation comes over me. One moment it's mild afternoon, the next it's chilly night. The world is upside down. The trees hang from the sky and nothing but darkness yawns beneath. Then as quickly as the image forms, it vanishes, and I stumble into daylight and drop to my knees in damp grass.

I blink to clear my vision and find Anna's hand hovering in front of my face. I let her help me up, surveying the small park we've appeared in.

"Not bad, first time tree traveler," she says.

"Thanks." I brush the dirt off my knees and check the tree. It looks completely normal, but I remember what Anna said about the trees being full of magic and wonder what else they can do.

"How did we get here?" I ask.

Anna nods at the trees. "This whole wood is Hollowthorn, the forest I was telling you about. A lot of magic comes through from the Otherworld because of the weak spot in the Shield, so these trees are full of it. We'll have to catch a taxi home, though. That's one-way travel. But we're close to downtown!"

Max leads us from the small grove and onto the sidewalk, Anna stepping merrily on the crunching leaves as we go. Several people do a double take when they see him walking with us, and he makes a point of doing something strange any time someone stares too long, like rearing back to walk on his hind paws. But just as many don't seem bothered by the cat at all, and I have a feeling they're the local magical folk.

Downtown Wick is more forest than town. Brightly colored cottages poke out from behind thick tree trunks and between blankets of red and gold leaves, and hardly any of the buildings rise above the canopy. There are few cars, mostly people walking bundled up in knit sweaters and woolen caps against the thickening mist. The whole place smells of earth after a rain.

Petrichor, I think.

I like it. For a moment, I dip into my old daydream, imagining my family and myself making a life here alongside the brightly colored buildings and the sound of the wind in the trees. Mom and Dad would love looking at all the little cottages, and Liam would take me exploring in the woods. Then I remember my parents are gone, and it snatches my breath away.

I've been trying not to think about them, just like I've been trying not to think about the fact that Liam hasn't arrived, but one of the men he was after is here now. Did they split up? Is Liam here tracking him, too, or did he go after the other one?

What if something happened to him and he never comes back?

He will, I tell myself. *He promised. And when he gets here, I'll have answers for him.*

A misty rain follows us the rest of the way to the main street, where Anna points to a row of round, pumpkin-shaped houses next door. "Those are the witches' cottages," she says. "The locals go to them for spells, and all of Willow Street is spelled for good luck. It's where most of the magical shops are."

I hope some of that luck rubs off on me as I scan the area, looking for anyone who resembles Kaden.

"And that shop sells magical hats," Anna continues, pointing at a dark green building covered in ivy. "Max gets a lot of the house's hats from there. Which reminds me—don't put any of the house's hats on."

Max nods his agreement.

I hear her, but I don't hear her, until she grabs my hand and tugs me toward a purple and white shop front with the name spelled out in real black flowers—THE WICKED ORCHID.

"What—Anna! We have to find Kaden."

"We don't know what he is or what he's capable of," she

62

replies, releasing my hand to push open the shop door. "My family knows a lot of the magical beings here, which makes me think he's something that can take another form. Maybe a shapeshifter or a demon. Whatever he is, though, we need to be prepared."

A flood of rose-scented air hits me, and we enter a greenhouse that's impossibly large inside compared to the outside. Eight panes of solid glass come to a point for the ceiling, and the shop floor is a mismatched jungle.

An older, brown-skinned teen wearing all black emerges from behind a wall of climbing ivy, a bundle of lavender clasped in her fingers, which are lined with different-colored rings. Thick eyeliner circles her brown eyes, and she wears forest-green lipstick. She glides toward us with an easy grace, ducking down to scratch Max under the chin with nails painted to resemble the night sky. The pinpricks of white stars actually move, arcing across her nails like shooting stars.

"Hey, Anna," she says with a smile. "Does Rose need more seedlings?"

"Hi, Dilara." Anna points at a wall to her left where a series of bracelets hang. They're all made of flowers and berries, some woven together, others tied in intricate knots. "Actually, can we just have two rowanberry bracelets?" she asks.

Dilara peers shrewdly at us. I get the feeling she knows something's up, but she nods toward the wall. Anna grabs two bracelets made of bright red berries strung together, slipping one onto her wrist and the other onto mine.

"Thank you! Can you put it on Rose's tab?"

"Is she going to ask me about it when I pick her up for our date tonight?" Dilara asks.

"It's Rose," Anna says, already retreating toward the door.

"She'll probably ask you about the emotional implications of what you had for breakfast. Gotta go now, sorry, bye!" She grabs my hand again, dragging me out of the store with Max on our tails.

I inspect the small berries, which are oddly warm against my skin. "What is this supposed to do?"

"Rowanberries ward off evil spirits and protect you from enchantments," Anna replies. "Since we don't know what Kaden is, hopefully these'll help keep us safe while we look for him. I'm betting if he's still here, he's somewhere on Willow Street."

We search the street, checking inside shops, ducking down allies, and peering through fences into backyards. There's a shop that grants wishes, and another that bottles dreams. My personal favorite is the store filled entirely with different sized and shaped candles that, when lit, help you relive memories.

None of the owners have seen Kaden, and we find no sign of him in the magical hat shop, the potion supply store, or the enchanted bakery, run by a witch who gives us each a bite-sized cream puff that tastes like sunshine. In all of them, tourists and nonmagical residents only occupy half the stores, as if they don't even realize the second halves are there, filled with magical items they could only dream of.

"Aren't you worried people will notice?" I ask when a couple completely ignores a set of floating cake stands in the bakery.

Anna shakes her head, her curls wet from the rain and sticking to her face. "A lot of magical people and creatures come to Wick because they're stronger here, and safer. They want to live peacefully with nonmagical people, and we all work together to keep our powers a secret while still staying in business."

"But the cakes." I gesture at the clearly floating tiers. "Are they glamoured?"

"Yup. All the magical shops here are. Those people just see normal cakes."

"Then why can I see them?" In fact, it hasn't just been the floating cakes. Everywhere we've gone, and at Ravenfall, too, I've had no trouble seeing the magical elements.

Anna's face scrunches up in confusion. "When someone's really open to magic, and knows to look for it, they can sometimes see through glamours. I guess you really are embracing the weird."

That should make me happy, but by the time we reach the last building on the lane with a sign that says ANDRADE ANIMAL SHELTER, my hope of finding Kaden has dwindled, and my mood along with it.

The shelter is a small green building with cartoon dogs and cats on the face and a big front window with the shade pulled down.

Anna stops halfway up the ramp with a frown. "The light's on in the front."

"So?"

Her hand strays to her rowanberry bracelet. "Only Mr. and Mrs. Andrade work the front, and they're at Ravenfall. So who's inside?"

I'm past her and to the door before she can call out, "Colin, *wait!*"

A bell rings above when I enter, and Max lets out a low growl. My gaze leaps across waiting room chairs and coffee tables piled with magazines to the front counter and the room beyond. If Kaden's in here, he'd have heard the bell, and—

Something moves behind the counter.

An older man in a crisp black suit with short, curly hair looks up from a stack of papers to smile at us, and I recognize him from the inn.

"Anna! What brings you by?" Mr. Andrade asks.

My disappointment swells, but Anna looks relieved. "Sorry, Mr. Andrade. We thought you were at Ravenfall, so we got concerned by the light."

"Well, I appreciate you checking. I just came by to look in on Elra—he's been a little on edge of late."

A tiny flying lizard shoots out from behind the counter and latches onto Anna's face. No, not a lizard—*a dragon*. About the size of my palm with iridescent scales and gossamer wings, the dragon clings to Anna's face in a hug, its miniscule pink tongue tickling her eyebrow.

She laughs, gathering the dragon into her hands. "Hi, Elra."

"Have you seen a man with blond hair and green eyes lurking around?" I ask hopefully. "He's about this tall, looks really mean."

Mr. Andrade shakes his head. "Can't say I have. I've only just come by. Elra might be able to help, though."

Anna's face lights up. "That's a great idea!" When all I do is stare at her, she holds the glittering dragon up. "Pocket dragons are great at finding things. You just have to touch him and give him an image to go off of."

I stare at the dragon. The dragon stares back. Max hisses at him.

Anna proffers me the dragon, and I take him with a sigh. His little body is shockingly cold to the touch, and his thin tail circles around my thumb. I focus on an image of Kaden, and the dragon begins to warm in my hands. Then he launches into the air and out the door, tongue flicking out to scent the air. Just as quickly he's in my hands again, and this time an image forms in my mind: a beautiful white bridge over a lazy river, surrounded by trees and fog.

I describe it to Anna, and she claps her hands together. "He's in the Faerie Garden. Let's go!"

We return Elra to Mr. Andrade with a thank-you and take off with Max down the street. The rain has picked up, coming down in a heavy drizzle.

Anna's voice takes on a nervous edge as we run. "What exactly is our plan here?"

My hands curl into fists, pumping at my sides. "Get some answers."

Make him pay for what he did. The thought surprises me, but I don't push it away. Whoever this guy is, the person he works for not only took my parents from me but might have taken my brother too. He destroyed my entire life, and I want to know why.

Anna looks concerned, but then my eyes catch on a painted sign over her shoulder that reads THE FAERIE GARDEN. It pokes out between two of the witches' cottages, the buildings casting long shadows over a gravel path that disappears into an expanse of trees.

We follow the path into a landscaped forest, where tufts of fog hang low to the ground and the only sound is the pluck of raindrops against leaves.

"The bridge is this way," Anna says, following a forking path to the right. The gravel turns to dirt as we pass through a maze of colors. Everything is cloaked in mist, making the plants and flowers look ghostly.

Through an arch made of intertwined branches, the path opens into a white wooden bridge wrapped in moss and dead vines. A willow hangs over it, its wispy branches haunting in the mist, and a strange clacking noise fills the air. Coming our way across the bridge is a man in a dark leather jacket, his blond hair stuck to his head by the drizzling rain.

Kaden.

He stops when he sees us, a serpentine smile cutting across his face that's nothing like the sleepy man from the photo. "I've been looking for you, boy," he growls. "And a Ballinkay, too, how perfect. He'll be mighty pleased to see you dead along with the Raven." He draws a knife from his belt.

Max hisses, his fur standing on end, and Anna makes a small noise of surprise. Not at the knife, but at what Kaden said. She repeats it under her breath. "A Raven?"

My hands flex at my sides, months of training itching to be used. Boxing, wrestling, grappling. Liam taught me a lot since we started moving, and at the moment I want nothing more than to unleash all of it on Kaden. He's on the small side, while I've always been big for my age.

"Careful, Colin," Anna says quietly. "Something's off about him."

"Who was the other man in the room with you?" I close the distance between us.

"My lord doesn't concern you," Kaden replies smoothly. He flips the knife around expertly so the butt of it faces his chest, ready to slash, and suddenly I don't feel so sure about this. Kaden might not be big, but he's still bigger than me, and I've never been in a fight with anyone other than Liam, and definitely not with a knife.

"Colin, I don't know about this," Anna says.

Some part of me knows she's right, but I can't walk away from this. Kaden is my only chance to get answers.

"What are you?" I demand. "Where's my brother?"

"You ask a lot of questions for dead folk," Kaden hisses. Then he lunges, slashing with the blade.

Control the knife first, Liam's voice commands. I catch Kaden's forearm with both hands, shoving away the knife as Anna falls back. My fist comes up lightning fast, catching him on the jaw with a hard hook. He stumbles back half a step, looking more surprised than hurt, and I feel the same shock on my face.

"I forgot you Pierces were fighters." He tests the spot on his face with his fingers. "Won't happen again."

He lunges, and this time I barely manage to duck and step away fast enough. He's on me immediately, too strong and quick. It's all I can do to stay away from him now.

This is nothing like sparring with Liam; this is real, and I'm no match for Kaden.

This was a mistake.

I leap away from the slash of his knife, and then Anna is there. At first I think she's going to grab him, but then I see a flash of red as she slides her rowanberry bracelet over Kaden's hand. He gasps as if she struck him. His form flickers once, twice, and then *changes.*

His skin turns bone white and withers like crumpled paper, and his face elongates, making room for rows of needle-thin teeth. His cheeks grow sunken, his eyes becoming bottomless black pits without a hint of white at the edges.

Anna backs away, her eyes blown wide with fear. "You're a wraith," she breathes.

"A what?" I ask.

"A spirit that's possessed a human body," she explains. "But then the berries—you should have been expelled from Kaden's body!"

Kaden laughs, the sound deep and rasping. "This body is mine, little Ballinkay."

He shoots forward and I push Anna back. Sharp claws clip my forearm; then Kaden grabs for my throat, but I'm too off balance to deflect it.

Something slams into me.

Anna and I hit the damp ground hard a second before a black shape flies over us. The bridge groans as Max completes his transformation, his massive, shadowy body filling the entire width of it. He lets out a rasping bellow somewhere between a dragon roaring and a lion hissing.

Kaden retreats. "This isn't over, Raven. We're coming for you on Samhain, and your pet Jabberwocky won't be able to save you then."

He bolts down the bridge, disappearing into the fog.

CHAPTER 9

Anna

When Max's body shrinks, revealing the bridge, Kaden is gone.

I try to catch my breath as I clamber to my feet and help Colin to his. He cringes when I grab his forearm where Kaden's claws cut him. I quickly let go, and he nearly tumbles back to the ground and pulls me with him.

"You okay?" I ask, wiping the blood I've gotten on my hands down the side of my pants.

"Yeah, it's just a scratch," he replies, before his whole face contracts in a frown. "Is Max?"

I spin around. Max is lying on his side, panting heavily. "Oh no!" I drop beside him, gathering him into my arms. "He was too far away from the house to shift. It drained his energy."

Standing, I dump him against Colin's chest. "I don't want him!" he exclaims, looking unsure of how to hold him.

"You're a Raven!" I snap back. "You're basically a walking Shield. Being close to you will restore his energy."

Colin blinks. "I'm a what?"

"Well, you're maybe a Raven," I mutter to myself, trying to wrap my mind around the possibility. I definitely didn't see this coming. There are so few left now that most magical communities rarely see them, and one hasn't lived in Wick in years. "That's according to Kaden, and he's not exactly trustworthy."

"Anna," Colin says flatly.

I wince, realizing he has no idea what I'm talking about. "Sorry! Ravens are keepers of the Shield. They hunt dangerous creatures whose actions might expose magic. Jabberwockies are usually connected to them, because they can't exist in the human world without a link to the Shield."

Max is unusual because he lives with us, not a Raven, and uses the energy of the house as his link to the Shield. Ravenfall is actually named after the first Jabberwocky to bond with a human thousands of years ago—and the Ravenguard name evolved from that.

I pace along the bridge, trying to make sense of things. "But if you're a Raven, that means your parents were too, and Liam. Now it turns out they were killed by something magical? There's no way this is a coincidence, Colin."

None of it is—Kaden being from Wick, Colin showing up at Ravenfall, now this? What's going on?

Colin leans against the railing, looking overwhelmed. Learning about magic is one thing; learning *you're* magical is another. Tack on the "hunted by a wraith and his boss" part and I'm surprised he's still standing.

"Are you okay?" I ask, coming to a stop.

"I think so," he says slowly. "It's just a lot to take in. I wish . . . I wish my parents had told me the truth about all this. I wish they'd prepared me . . ." He trails off, his face clouding with anger. "I hate that they're not here to help me now. They should be teaching me all this stuff."

I try a reassuring smile, but I've never been any good at them. Something about looking like I stepped on a nail. At least, that's what Kara says.

"I'm sorry," I try instead, and it's enough to make Colin's expression soften.

He runs a frustrated hand through his hair. "They always told me that we were in witness protection, and that's why we had to move all the time. But if this is all true, then what if we were really running from Kaden and whoever he works for? This might be the first step in figuring out why he killed them."

"It would also explain what Kaden said before he ran," I add, putting the pieces together. "About coming after you on Samhain."

Before he can answer, a metallic noise slides through the air, and I realize with a sinking feeling where exactly we are. Golden eyes watch us from the willow tree, glowing unnaturally, and the air grows heavy with a coppery scent.

I move closer to Colin. "Let's get out of here. This bridge belongs to a redcap."

"A what?"

"Irish creature. Kills things, soaks its cap in the blood of its victims. Not real friendly."

Colin's face pales, and I tow him quickly across the bridge. "Let's go talk to Gran. Maybe she can tell us something about what Kaden was doing here."

I lead the way through the park and back to the sidewalk of

Willow Street. The Faerie Garden is one of my favorite places to come and draw—the bridge aside, of course—and I know its paths inside and out. I never come by without stopping in the Merrow a few houses down, and Gran *always* knows when I'm nearby.

As we walk, I glance sidelong at Colin, who seems withdrawn. Wraiths are scary, and it was really brave of him to try and take Kaden on, even if he turned out to be too much. I want to tell him that, but then I worry he'll think I'm consoling him for losing. Why is this talking thing so hard?

The Merrow Café is in an old Victorian home painted scarlet and nestled in a group of cherry trees. The small pink and white flowers litter the thick lawn, gathering in puddles of rainwater. On the café porch, a humongous dog with a midnight-green coat so dark it looks black lies with its head propped on its paws. Max hisses at it as we near, and it lifts its boxy head.

"Sorry, Mr. Connolly," I say. "He's in a bad mood."

The dog's eyes flash red, and Colin sucks in a breath. I drag him past the cù-sìth and into the café, where the delicious smell of Gran's fresh baked brown bread greets us.

The Merrow is empty, tending to draw most of its crowd from the Faerie Garden visitors who are absent with the falling rain. An L-shaped counter takes up most of the front room, laden with trays of strawberry and oatmeal cream scones, baskets of peanut butter chocolate chip cookies, and hundreds of tiny glass jars of different types of tea.

Gran's tea is known all over Wick for the way it makes people feel. Honey lavender tea relaxes the drinker's worries, and caramel rooibos renews old memories. My favorite is the Earl Grey vanilla, which gives pleasant dreams drawn from the drinker's wishes.

Gran emerges behind the counter from the kitchen. "Anna-love!" She always attaches *love* at the end of my name like it's a part of it.

At first glance, she's every bit the sweet old woman, but bits of her wrinkled white skin are decorated in Celtic tattoos, and her silver hair is done up in a wild bun, the tips dyed fire red.

"Hi, Gran." I smile as she comes to our side of the counter to kiss my cheek. No kiss, no food.

Colin starts to offer his hand. "Hi, I'm—"

But Gran already has him in her arms. I know from experience there's nothing better than a hug from her, and Colin melts into it. Gran looks like she might cry, but only steps back with a sad smile.

"I know who you are, lad," she says gently. "Nora called me last night. A shame to hear about your parents, it was."

Colin draws himself up, and he reminds me of the boy getting out of the taxi again, trying so hard to look older. "It's nice to meet you, Mrs. Ballinkay."

"Call me Gran, dear," she says, grabbing a clean cloth and tossing it to him. He cradles Max in one arm in order to catch it. "I only wish we'd met under different circumstances. Your parents were some of the finest people I knew, may their souls find peace."

Colin clutches Max a little closer, but for the most part, he seems okay. Unlike me, Gran always knows what to say.

"We're going to go sit down, Gran," I say, guiding Colin through the narrow hall to the back room.

"Food will be up soon, Anna-love!" she calls.

"We didn't order anything," Colin says as the hall opens into a cozy sitting area. There are small, mismatched tables scattered around with rose-light candles. Bookcases surround the room, most filled to the brim with an array of mismatched teacups and saucers, the others lined with age-old spell books, journals, and bottles of whiskey older than Gran. Local artists have their work up for sale all over and I scan the pieces as we walk. A drawing of a selkie flicks its tail at us.

I lead Colin to my favorite sketching table in the corner beside the fireplace, which simmers with an enchanted peat fire. If you know how to look for it, the flames will show you faraway lands, but I don't think what Colin needs right now is more magic. Beside us, the candle-laden window overlooks an outdoor seating area, which seems as if it grew out of the ground together with the vines and flowers. Considering Gran's many witch friends, it might have.

"No one orders here," I reply, giving Colin the chair nearest the fire. "Gran knows what you want better than you do."

"Is she psychic too?" he asks, laying Max down gently in his lap. He finally seems to realize what the towel is for and turns his arm over to inspect the wound. The scratch is shallow and has stopped bleeding, so he cleans it off and wraps his arm in the towel.

I shrug, trying to wrangle my frizzed curls into a semblance of a bun. It takes me three tries. "Yeah, but no one knows what exactly she can do other than telekinesis. You can ask her if you want, but she'll just pretend she didn't hear you."

Colin's frown takes over his face. "We didn't come here for food. We need answers."

"And it'll take even longer to get them if you try to turn down Gran's cooking. It's best just to let her feed us, then ask questions."

Gran appears in the hallway, a tray of food floating after her.

We each get a heaping bowl of chicken and dumplings with buttered brown bread on the side, and an oatmeal butterscotch muffin, which Colin stares at hungrily. Cups of tea come zipping over from the counter: cardamom rose for the both of us, to ward off inner chills and frights.

I catch Gran up as we eat, ending with the fight in the garden and what we learned. "Kaden said Colin is a Raven. Is that true?" I ask through a mouthful of brown bread.

"Swallow your food before you speak, Anna-love," Gran chastises softly. "And yes, it is. The power of a Raven is passed down through generations, and both your mother and father were of ancient lines."

Colin sits with that for a moment, his spoon balanced on the bowl's edge. "Do you think . . ." He takes a deep breath. "Do you think that's why Kaden and his employer killed them? Because they're—we're—Ravens?"

Gran folds her hands together and sets her chin atop them. "That is very possible."

"He was strong, Gran," I say, remembering the odd feeling of power I'd sensed from Kaden. "I got a string of rowanberries around his wrist, and it didn't expel him. He said—" I stop, the pieces sliding into place. "He said the body was his! That's why the rowanberries didn't work. I think he absorbed the real Kaden's soul."

I'd heard of it before—permanent possessions, where no amount of magic could ever free the victim of its invading spirit. But I'd never actually seen it.

Gran's face grows grim. "This is worse than I thought. The spirit possessing Kaden would have to be extremely powerful to manage that, and we would know if the Shield had broken down enough to let something that strong through. I suspect whoever he works for must have helped him, which would make him a formidable foe."

I dip my bread in the last of my soup and take a bite. "He said—" Gran shoots me a pointed look, and I close my mouth, chewing quickly and swallowing. "He said he was looking for Colin. I think that's why he was downtown. But how did he know to come to Wick?"

"The real Kaden is from here, and the wraith has access to his memories," Gran replies. "I wouldn't be surprised if he knew your parents or knew of them, and thought you might come here for safety."

"He was right," Colin mutters. "Do you think he knows I'm at Ravenfall?"

"He does now that he's seen you with Anna." Gran spins one finger, and a teaspoon stirs sugar into her tea on its own. "But not to worry, he won't be able to get past the house's wards once it knows to keep him out. Also, does your mother know where you've gone?"

I grin nervously and take a large bite of brown bread, chewing extra slow.

"I didn't think so." Gran reclines in her chair, folding her arms.

"Who would a wraith be working for?" Colin asks, scraping his bowl for every last bit of food.

"Wraiths are spirits that have crossed over and possessed a living body," Gran replies. "Their motivations will be attached to whoever they were in life."

Colin's fingers curl around his bowl, and Gran gives him a look that clearly says, *Mind the dishware.* He forces out a deep breath.

"Colin is sure he saw Kaden's boss's face, but he can't remember it," I say.

Gran's brow furrows. "Sounds like a glamour. If you're aware of it and you look hard enough, you can see through it."

Colin looks vaguely ill. "And now that ultra-powerful being knows that I'm staying at Ravenfall. Kaden said he was coming after me on Samhain. You're all in danger because of me."

"Not to worry, we can handle ourselves," Gran says with a wink.

"Yeah," I agree. "We'll figure out who he works for and why they're after you, Colin. I promise."

Gran nods. "Not to mention, you are very well-warded, so it will be difficult for Kaden to find you outside of Ravenfall. You'll be safe inside the inn."

We finish our soup and Colin goes for his muffin. He tries a little and makes a satisfied sound. Then he takes a giant bite out of the rest.

Gran lets out a dry laugh. "Didn't know there was another soul alive who loves butterscotch as much as Anna. You'd best savor that muffin; it's the best you'll ever have."

"I don't know, my mom's were pretty great," he says when he finishes chewing.

Gran scoffs. "And where do you think she got the recipe, my boy?" She flourishes a hand.

Colin gawks, and Gran laughs again. "Your mother worked here during the summers. In fact, this is where she met your father. He was in from the East Coast tracking a rare type of faerie."

Colin's face goes slack as Gran launches into the story of his parents meeting, and by the time he's coaxed several more stories out of her, the rain has slowed down and something heavy has slipped from Colin's shoulders. His face looks a little less pale, his shoulders a little looser. I wonder if it has anything to do with the three cups of tea Gran made him drink. Or maybe just talking about his parents helped.

We finish our lunch and say goodbye to Gran, who sends us off in a taxi with a half-dozen oatmeal butterscotch muffins.

CHAPTER 10

Colin

I'm so wrapped up in thinking about everything I've learned that I only realize we're at Ravenfall when Max's tail smacks me in the face on his way out of the taxi. He'd been curled up in my jacket, still lethargic. The driver makes a small noise of protest when Max exits, obviously not having realized the cat was there.

Anna peers in at me, looking concerned. I must be really gloomy if even she can tell something's wrong, but I can't shake myself out of it. For months my family and I jumped city to state to town, and now I finally know what we were running from. All this time my parents hid the truth from me, and not just them, but Liam too.

I never asked why he snuck out at night. Never asked why he came home with scabbed knuckles and bruised ribs. I thought he just needed some space, needed to blow off some steam. But now the strangeness of it all makes sense. The tufts of fur I found in the trunk of the car, the strange silver spots on his clothes that I dismissed as paint.

All this time he was out hunting.

I'm the only one who didn't know, and it makes me feel stupid. I should have seen it. I should have been prepared. My parents should have taught me how to defend myself—not just with random boxing lessons from Liam, but with real knowledge of what we are—and now they'll never teach me anything again.

And the worst part is, I still don't even know why.

As my anger wells inside me, I hold my breath until my throat burns, then let it out in a rush and clamber out of the vehicle. My body feels tired and heavy, and I don't move as the taxi pulls around the circular drive and heads toward town.

Then I see the car.

There's no mistaking the '67 Dodge Charger parked to the side of the inn. It's bright as a beacon with its marigold paint, the sides and hood detailed in maroon flames that my dad did himself, to my mom's never-ending horror. Seeing it now is like running into a teacher out of class—it doesn't belong here.

Unless . . .

"Colin?" Anna asks uncertainly.

I move toward the car just as the driver's door opens, my heart soaring—but it isn't Liam who gets out.

A short, thin woman with blue braids emerges, clutching a clipboard. My heart plummets, and suddenly I feel sick. As she approaches, something tells me I should run, that I shouldn't listen to what she has to say.

But then she's standing before me and her soft voice is asking, "You Colin Pierce?"

I nod mechanically. She holds out the clipboard. "Sign here for delivery."

"Delivery from who?" Anna regards her suspiciously.

She shrugs. "Couldn't say. The car was left at our lot with instructions to deliver it to a Colin Pierce at Ravenfall Inn should it remain unclaimed, and let me tell you, this place isn't easy to find."

Unclaimed. The word reverberates in my head. *Unclaimed.*

There's only one reason the car would be unclaimed.

Anna must see my rising panic, because she steps between the woman and me so that I'm looking at her. "There are a lot of reasons Liam might not have gotten the car," she says. "We don't know what happened."

The driver proffers the clipboard impatiently over Anna's shoulder. I take it, signing without looking, and she exchanges it for the car keys. A taxi rumbles up the driveway, and she waves it down. Then she's gone, leaving me clutching the cold metal keys to my chest.

"Colin?" Anna asks quietly.

"I don't even have a picture of him. Of any of them." My parents had made us leave everything but the necessities at home when we left. I hadn't thought to grab a photo—I hadn't realized what was happening. The only phones they'd let us have since then were cheap burners with cameras older than Ravenfall. My old cell phone got smashed along with anything else trackable.

My hand closes around the Irish knot charm at my neck, the metal warm from the heat of the cab. As a kid, when I couldn't sleep at night, my mother used to loop it around my neck and tell me it was a magical talisman that would protect me. Now the necklace and the car are all I have left of them.

"I should have been there. Why didn't they tell me about any of this? I could have—" I stop. "I feel so stupid."

Anna shakes her head. "You're not stupid. Your family was trying to protect you."

"But *I* could have protected them!" Our parents did everything for us. Worked, took care of me and Liam, kept a roof over our heads even after we started moving around. And on top of that, they were also protecting us from a whole other world? I can't help but think of every time I didn't listen to them or got upset. They didn't deserve it.

"Now they're gone," I say softly. "They're all gone."

"Family doesn't end with death," Anna says with one of her terrible reassuring smiles. "They're still there for you, just not in the way you might think."

I almost laugh. Only Anna would think ghosts are a comforting thought. Something leans into my leg, and I look down to find Max's tail curving around it.

"And you're not alone," she adds. "It'll be okay."

The words flip a switch, and my anger dies. It's such a normal thing to say, and yet I needed to hear it. Liam said it to me a thousand times, his unyielding optimism sometimes more frustrating than our situation. Even as we sat on the side of the road eating cheap burgers and soggy fries, he'd say it. *It'll be okay.*

Optimism. Hopefulness and confidence about the future.

We have new information about Kaden and the man he works for. We made it back safely.

And I'm not alone.

Anna leads me toward the house, Max trotting at my heel. The front door swings open on its own, and we've barely taken a step inside when a voice rings out. "Annabella Neviah Ballinkay!"

Nora's in the kitchen with her hands on her hips. Max takes one look at her and bolts back out the front door. I wish I could follow—she has the exact same *you're in so much trouble* look on her face my mom would get.

Anna shrinks as if she might disappear into her sweater. "Yes?"

"Gran called. You went after a wraith?"

"Um, it was an accident?"

Before Nora can respond, another voice booms, "Anna? Is that you?" A bear of a man emerges from inside the kitchen. His features are soft and kind, melding together as he grins.

"Uncle Roy!" Anna goes to hug him, but he beats her to it, scooping her up and lifting her off her feet. He spins her once and sets her down with a laugh.

"I'm so glad you're home!" she exclaims. "I'm surprised the house let you in."

Roy grins. "We've come to an understanding." He pats the wall and the paint comes away on his hand, where parts of his pale skin are wrinkled and red with old burn scars. He makes a face and wipes his hand down his pant leg.

"Did you bring me anything from Ireland?" Anna asks hopefully.

Roy barks a laugh. "Again? I'm here nearly every month!"

Anna folds her arms. "It's my payment for making sure the house doesn't throw out all your stuff." The house groans, as if announcing that it'd love to do just that.

"Roy," Nora interjects. "This isn't—"

Roy's voice cuts across hers. "You must be Colin," he says to me. I hold out my hand. "It's nice to meet you."

He takes it in a firm grip, though his palms are soft and cushiony. "Roy Ballinkay, but you can call me Uncle Roy. Come sit down, Colin!"

He tugs my hand, and the rest of my body comes flying after it, forcing me to take a few quick steps to keep my feet under me. Anna darts after us as we turn into the room opposite the kitchen.

Shelves of books line three of the walls, the fourth a patchwork of different-sized windows overlooking the Hollowthorn Woods beyond. Worn leather sofas sit beside a simmering peat fire, and all I want is to grab a stack of books and sink into one. I'm so distracted by the books I almost don't notice the different style hats hanging on the face of the mantel, from an Irish baseball cap to a dusty bowler hat straight out of an old movie.

A tray with five cups sits on a high table behind one couch, the orange scent of Earl Grey filling the air as a gleaming silver pot pours tea.

Nora surges in after us. "Roy! I wasn't finished with them."

I sink into the couch as Anna counts the teacups and then the four of us.

"Oh, right." Roy folds his arms across his barrel chest, doing his best to look disapproving.

Anna grins sheepishly at Nora. "Maybe we didn't think it through."

"Or at all." Elaine strides into the room and straight for a cup of tea. "Did Gran send anything home?"

"Don't change the subject!" Nora swats at her. I lower the box of muffins I'd been about to offer Elaine. "Kaden's boss will be coming for you now, too, Anna. For all of us. Do you realize the danger you've put this family in?"

I knew it. Gran tried to reassure me, but I've put Anna's whole family in danger. I'm as much a burden to them as I was my own family.

"I'm sorry," I say, standing. "It's my fault we went after the wraith, and it's my fault you're all in danger now. I should go."

Roy's hand falls on my shoulder and I drop back down. "You're not going anywhere, lad." He hands me a cup of tea. "Your father's ghost would haunt me to the end of days if I let you walk out that door."

"Besides, Colin's in danger!" Anna says.

All eyes fall on me and I straighten. Nora worries at her mouth, and Elaine shifts uncomfortably. There's something they're not telling us.

Anna frowns suspiciously. "You knew, didn't you? You knew he was a Raven?"

Nora sighs, running a hand through her hair. "Yes, we did."

I set my teacup down. "Why didn't you tell me?"

Nora hesitates; then the tension washes out of her like water wrung from a rag. She takes the last cup of tea, joining me and Anna on the couch.

"You had a lot to take in yesterday as it was," she tells me. "And we weren't sure yet if their deaths were related to the Ravenguard. Your parents didn't want anything to do with magic anymore after Liam was born. They wanted normal lives for you both, so much so that they cut ties with us." Her voice tightens, and Roy shifts nervously in the silence, almost looking . . . guilty?

"We were only respecting their wishes," she finishes.

Frustration flares inside me. "What about my wishes? My parents are dead because of a secret nobody would tell me!"

The room is silent, but my anger still feels ready to burst out of me. I'm so tired of being lied to, of being in the dark. First my parents, then Liam, now the Ballinkays. No one ever considers what I want—they just choose for me, and I'm tired of it.

I hold my breath, forcing my emotions away. I have to stay in control. Mature. If they think I can't handle this, if they think I'm just a kid, they'll keep more from me.

"I need to know the truth," I say more calmly. "I can't handle any more lies."

"Very well," Nora says, and my heart leaps. "Ravens channel the Shield's power into magic and abilities that they use to protect people from everything from evil spirits to demons. It's a dangerous job, which is why your parents wanted out of the life when Liam was born."

When I arrived at Ravenfall looking for answers, I never imagined this is what I'd get. The last day has been enough to convince me everything they're saying is true, yet it still feels impossible, as though someone's pulled aside a curtain that's been there all my life.

"They hunted supernatural creatures?" I ask.

"They were some of the best we knew at it," Elaine says fondly. A faint smile tugs at her lips. "Bridget once took on a fully grown redcap with her bare hands. And your father, he—" She cuts off with a sad laugh. "Maybe I'll save that for when you're older."

Roy rubs her back comfortingly. "I still can't believe they're gone. Why didn't they reach out to us? We could have helped."

"Maybe they didn't think they could," Nora says quietly. "After how things ended between us."

Roy looks away, and Elaine traces the skull tattoo on her forearm. "That wouldn't have mattered."

There's something surreal about listening to them talk about my parents like this. As though they're not my parents at all, but two entirely different people who led entirely different lives. It makes me sad to think that I might not have ever really known them.

"You said you weren't sure *yet* if their deaths had anything to do with them being Ravens." Anna studies them all over her teacup. "Does that mean you are now?"

Nora nods, her face grim once more. "We reached out to some friends. It turns out that other Ravens have been attacked the last few months, and a few have died. The attacks were getting more frequent recently, but it's been quiet since the death of your parents."

"I was able to contact one of the Raven's spirits," Elaine adds. "They confirmed whoever killed them used only his hands, but they also couldn't remember his face. Memories get slippery after you move on."

"Someone is hunting us," I say as understanding settles. "This wasn't just about my parents."

"We believe so," Elaine agrees. "It also explains the flood of ghosts the night you arrived, Colin. The Shield had been waning for some time as the population of Ravens naturally declined over generations, but with the sudden deaths of so many, the Shield has been fading in and out so close to Samhain."

"I saw a wisp the morning before you arrived," Anna adds. "Normally they don't show up until closer to Samhain, but it must have slipped through with the Shield weakened."

"What we don't know," Elaine continues, "is why you're being hunted or who's doing it."

A flame leaps to life in Roy's palm. "We're gonna have words when I find out, though."

A window behind him opens, letting in a wind to put out the flame, and he grins sheepishly at the house. I'd forgotten he'd have a power too, and the ability to control flames explains the burn scars on his arms. That had to be hard to learn to use.

"Kaden said that they'd be coming for Colin on Samhain," Anna says thoughtfully. "Do you think it's related?"

"I'm sure it is," Nora says, before catching my confused

expression. "Samhain is when the Shield is thinnest, allowing weaker spirits to cross over. They're also more powerful when they're here, capable of doing things they wouldn't be otherwise. A lot of magical beings are stronger on Samhain, including Ravens. Whatever Kaden's boss is planning, it makes sense it'd come to fruition on Samhain, and it explains why the attacks were speeding up the closer it got."

Roy rubs his hands together, creating a trail of smoke. "Which leaves us just under two weeks to teach you to use your abilities."

"My abilities?" I look between him and Nora, whose face has gone pale.

"Absolutely not, Roy," she says. "We're not involving him in this any more than he already is."

"He's already in it, Nor." Roy's voice softens. "They're targeting him, and he needs to know how to defend himself."

Elaine nods her agreement, and Nora's lips press into a thin line. I stare at her hopefully. These powers are my parents' legacy, one of the last things I have left tying me to them, and I know in that moment that no matter what Nora says, I'll find a way to learn more about them.

Nora winces, pressing a hand to her head in a sign I've realized means she's having a vision. Then she says, "It appears I don't really have a choice," and I wonder if she saw me learning to use my powers myself. "Very well. But on one condition."

"Anything," I say.

"You and Anna must never leave Ravenfall without supervision again until this matter is resolved. Kaden will be looking for you."

Anna makes a small noise of complaint, but I only nod. "Deal."

"In the meantime," Nora says, "I'm going to reach out to some other Ravens to spread the word and see if anyone has more information on who's behind this. Someone has to know something."

Elaine pushes off the couch. "Did your parents leave you a journal of some kind?"

I think of the blank notebook tucked away in my emergency bag that's not supposed to be there. Had they put it in my bag by mistake, or had they meant to finally tell me the truth? "I think so. It's upstairs."

"Bring it with you to the backyard tomorrow morning."

Anna's brow furrows. "Why? What's the journal got to do with anything?"

A popping noise sounds as Roy cracks his knuckles. He and Elaine exchange zealous looks, and Anna cringes, leaning close. "It's never a good sign when those two get along," she whispers.

Roy laughs. "This is going to be fun."

Tomorrow morning I'm to report to the backyard for training, but for tonight, I sneak outside to the Charger for some much-needed time to think.

The car smells of days-old food and stale pine air freshener. The driver's seat is still set to Liam's taller build, and my feet don't reach the pedals. I asked him to teach me to drive more than once, and he always told me the car was finicky and required a seasoned hand. Then he'd throw it into drive and slam on the accelerator, making the hinges of the seat screech as I was thrown into the seat. I secretly hoped that he'd get pulled over for it, but he never did. My brother was his own kind of magic.

Is, I tell myself. *He is.*

Looking back, I can't believe I never figured any of this out. Liam used to sneak out all the time, even once we started moving. He'd get in huge fights with Mom and Dad about it. They said they didn't want him hunting, but I always thought they meant animals.

I asked him about it once, and he'd looked sad when he told me, "I'd never hurt an innocent animal."

It hadn't made sense to me then, but now I think he was trying to tell me the truth in his own way.

I run my hands along the cold steering wheel, trying to find the places where my mother's fingers wore off the varnish, staining it dark.

I want to understand why they didn't tell me about all of this, but I don't know how to. They lied to me my entire life, and in the end, that lie is what killed them. If only they'd asked the Ballinkays for help. We could have come to Ravenfall as a family.

But I know my parents. They would have wanted to handle it on their own. They wouldn't have wanted to endanger anyone else, no matter what went down between them and the Ballinkays when they decided to leave the magical life behind.

Liam would know what happened. Liam always had answers. Only now he's one of my largest questions.

"Hurry up and come back," I whisper to the night. "Please."

CHAPTER 11

Colin

I'm up before the sun and waiting in the backyard with Anna, my parents' leather journal clutched in my hand.

The crisp autumn air is chilly but refreshing, and I breathe it in deep. The inn is quiet, the guests still asleep, and Anna has the day off from chores since it's Saturday. The grass is dotted with fallen leaves, and I can hear Max pouncing from one to the other as Anna dares him to leap farther and farther. Her sweater today is burnt orange with two black crows and reads ATTEMPTED MURDER.

Something flutters in the wind, and I blink, startled. "Anna?"

"Mmm?"

"Is that a . . . *hat* on your chimney?"

She follows my gaze to where a 1900s-style fedora with a gold feather balances on the gray stones. Smoke puffs merrily from the chimney, making the feather flutter.

"Oh," she says, clutching a half-empty mug of hot chocolate with pumpkin marshmallows to her chest. "The house likes them.

93

I'm pretty sure Max owes it big-time for something, because he takes a different hat up there every day."

I'd only been half listening when she talked about the hat shop downtown, but I remember her warning now not to put them on. Sometimes I wonder if I'll ever get used to this place.

The kitchen door opens, and Elaine and Roy emerge with cups of steaming coffee. Both are practically walking zombies, with deep purple bags under their eyes.

"We were out late last night canvasing the town for signs of Kaden," Roy explains to my questioning look. "No luck."

"Do you think he left?" Anna asks hopefully. "Or is he just biding his time until Samhain?"

"Liam really wounded his boss," I tell her. "Maybe he's taking care of him? That would explain why they aren't attacking until Samhain. Maybe he needs time to recover, and he'll be strong enough to fight on Samhain."

"Could be." Elaine yawns, then takes a huge sip of coffee. "Nora's heading into town this morning to ask around with Gran. Maybe they'll turn something up."

It makes me nervous not knowing what Kaden's up to, but right now, the only thing I can do is focus on learning how to use my powers.

"Can I see the journal?" Elaine holds out her hand, where a spiderweb tattoo traces the veins of her wrist, each line transitioning smoothly into looping cursive up her muscled bicep.

I offer it reluctantly, feeling oddly possessive.

"Yup, this is a true-blue Raven journal," she says, tracing the trinity knot with her finger.

"Raven journal?" I ask.

"They're special notebooks that belong to Ravens," Elaine

responds. When she flips it open, only blank pages stare back. "Have you bonded with it?"

"Bonded?"

Her entire forehead arches upward and she takes on a reciting tone. "These journals store power they gather from all sorts of magical sources. There are several ways for a Raven to awaken their magic, but the simplest is to bond with the journal."

"Elaine's a magical researcher," Anna says to my impressed look. Now *that* sounds like a career I could get behind.

"I think the term you're looking for is *know-it-all*," Roy says as his cooling coffee suddenly starts steaming at twice the rate.

Elaine ignores him and points to the trinity knot on the cover. "Put your hand on the cover and repeat after me." I do as she says, spreading my palm across the symbol.

She begins a spell in Irish, speaking slowly and enunciating each word as carefully as she can, and I do my best to repeat them. By the time she finishes, nothing's happened, and I feel foolish. Did they make a mistake? Maybe my parents never told me about their past because I didn't inherit their Raven powers.

Then the trinity symbol begins to glow.

She lets go, but the journal stays stuck to my hand. The light twirls around my fingers, snaking its way in little rivulets around my wrist and up my arm. It feels buzzy and warm.

"Effervescent," I mutter to myself.

"What?" Anna asks.

I grin. "Fizzy. That's how it feels."

Then the light reaches my shoulder and dives into the spot above my heart.

I gasp, expecting pain, but it's as gentle as a breeze. The light fades and the journal drops to the grass.

I start to ask what happened but stop when I realize I can feel it. I can feel *everything*. The air smells crisper, colder, full of rain to come. I can hear the wind now, not just the rustling leaves.

And the colors—everything around the house was already majestic, but now it's like someone slapped a filter on an image, supercharging it all.

My senses aren't the only things that have changed. I can feel the strength coiled inside me, waiting to be used. I flex my fingers, and they move so fast I would have missed it if not for my improved vision.

"Yup, it worked." Elaine gestures at the collection of black lines peeking up over my collar. I pull it down, revealing the Irish trinity knot now tattooed above my heart.

And at my feet, the journal is full of words.

"You feel different," Anna says. "I can feel your magic now, like Hollowthorn's or the house's."

"I can feel it too." I flex my fingers again, then poke the tattoo below my collarbone. "My dad had one just like this. I drew a copy of it on myself once with permanent marker and he got so mad . . ." I trail off as the pieces slot into place. "My parents were bonded to this before, weren't they?"

Elaine nods solemnly. "Families often share a journal. When its current owner dies, the journal relocates to the next closest relative. I'd wager that's how it ended up with you."

My hand falls to my side, my throat bobbing. "But then shouldn't it have gone to Liam?"

Roy and Elaine exchange worried looks. "You still haven't heard from him?" Elaine asks.

When I shake my head, Roy drops a reassuring hand on my shoulder. "There are a lot of reasons the journal might have come to you and not him. If it couldn't reach him, for example. There might be powerful magic blocking him."

I want to believe him, but between this, the car, and the fact that Liam still hasn't so much as called, I know that something is definitely wrong.

I clench my fist, trying to focus on my new magic and not my fear, and take a deep breath. "This is going to take some getting used to."

"That's why we're here," Roy says with a grin, tossing a flame between his palms. "Before you know it, your magic'll be just another part of you." The flame leaps into the air, does a little spin, and disperses in an impressive sparkler show.

Anna mock claps, and he bows.

"I'm going to drill you in hand-to-hand combat," he continues. "And Lady Bookworm here is going to help you with your magic."

"What do you two know about training Ravens?" Anna looks questioningly between them.

Elaine smiles. "We grew up with Colin's mom."

"I used to get Bridget into all kinds of trouble," Roy says wistfully. "Until Ma made me start training with her as an outlet for my, uh, emotions."

Elaine rolls her eyes. "You mean your temper?"

Roy slings an arm over her shoulders. "Still mad about that bedspread?"

"You set it on fire!" Elaine pushes his arm off. "Do you know how long that took me to make? If it weren't for that ghost I'd been chatting with, my whole room would have gone up in flames."

I try to imagine my mom hanging out with the Ballinkays. It's surreal to hear them talk about her like this. They had whole lives together once, lives I'll never hear them talk about thanks to Kaden and his boss.

A little of that anger comes flaring back, and I peer down at my hands as if I can see the power swirling in my veins. Up until now, I've been waiting for Liam to return, hoping I'll have information for him when I do. But now I have the power to do something myself.

The next time I see Kaden, I won't just be asking questions.

Animosity, I think. *Deep-seated dislike or ill will.*

Rancor. Enmity.

Revenge.

All words for the feeling roaring to life inside me. But first I need to learn how to use my powers.

"Anyway," Elaine says, turning her back on Roy's apologetic grin. "As I said, bonding to the journal awakened your magic. It was there before, but dormant."

"Think fast." Roy tosses a rock at me. I snatch it out of the air lightning fast, marveling at my own speed.

"Enhanced reflexes, speed, and strength are part of the basic Raven package," Roy says. "Your powers will grow stronger the older you get."

"What's this for, then?" Anna peers down at the journal. "Other than awakening his powers. And why couldn't he read it before?"

The pages are unlined and crammed full of cursive in various hands, plopped in at every angle to fill the space. Bits of paper and folded notes are taped onto the edges, and the bottom right corner boasts a drawing of a floating, ghostly ball of light, pulsing like a beacon.

Elaine picks up the journal. "A lot of Ravens glamour their

journals. If I remember right, your parents had a particularly tricky one on this. It was glamoured so you could only read it if you knew what it was."

She flips through the pages to show us different drawings. Each page is dedicated to a topic, from dealing with faeries and dybbukim to cultivating the most potent rowanberries.

"These journals are magical, and they're full of information on everything from supernatural creatures to spells to herbology," she explains. "Whatever information that family's line has gathered ends up here, and each member of the family bonds to it, then uses it on hunts and to store magical objects."

"Store?" I ask. "How?"

"Think of this less as a journal and more as a link to another dimension," Elaine says. "You're connected." She stops on a page with a detailed drawing of an amulet. There's a sprawling, thick-rooted tree carved into it.

"Dad brought one of those home once!" Anna exclaims. "He said they let people with magic cross the Shield into the Otherworld."

"And it's . . . inside the journal?" I ask uncertainly. It still feels strange to talk about this stuff as though it's real, and not out of a book.

"Yep." Elaine practically beams with excitement. "You just have to reach in and grab it."

"What?"

"Reach in and grab it," Elaine repeats, as if it's that simple and above all, normal.

I look between her and Roy's expectant expressions. They haven't led me wrong yet, so I do as they say and reach toward the page.

My fingers go straight through the paper, deeper than the depth of the journal, and I jerk away with a yelp.

Anna peers closer. "What? Did it bite?"

"No," I reply warily, still spooked by the empty space my hand found on the other side. "I just wasn't prepared for that."

"Try again!"

I reach in quicker this time, my fingers cutting through empty space to knock into something solid. Seizing it, I withdraw a smooth oak pendant, the symbol of the tree of life burned into the wood. We both gape at it, and I turn it over wonderingly in my hand.

"To return it, you just do the reverse." Elaine holds up the journal for me, where a blank space now waits. I place the amulet inside, and when I remove my hand, the drawing reappears on the page.

Anna grins. "That is so cool!" She snatches the journal out of Elaine's hand, flipping furiously through the pages. "What else is in here?"

"A lot, I'd wager," Roy says. "Like Elaine said, these journals are passed down within families, gathering power and magic the older they get. When two Ravens get married, they often combine their journals, so you're looking at the product of two powerful ancient lines: the Pierces and the O'Donnells. All the information they've gathered, all the supernatural creatures they've encountered, histories of their hunts, magical objects—it's in there. And we're going to walk you through it."

An entire history of my family, answers to questions I never knew to ask, and more information and research than I can imagine. Anna makes a face at the idea of walking through it all, but I can't wait to sit down and scan each page.

"Where do we start?" I ask with a grin.

CHAPTER 12

Anna

Anticipation bubbles through me. It's been a while since something magical surprised me, but the only Raven I ever knew was my dad's friend Salem, so I know about as much as Colin does now.

Uncle Roy cracks his knuckles with a grin. "We'll start with the basics. The main weapon in any Raven's arsenal is the ability to fight. We'll begin with some drills and see what you know; then I'll turn you over to Elaine to practice with the journal."

"What can I do?" I ask.

"Don't you have chores?" Aunt Elaine asks suspiciously.

"It's Saturday!" Still, the question deflates my excitement. Even Aunt Elaine's first thought when it comes to me is chores.

Uncle Roy and Colin are already off to the side going through a warm-up. I try to think of something useful to say or do, but I feel like a toadstool in a bed of roses and just end up standing there with the journal clutched to my chest, feeling more useless by the second.

Colin does everything Uncle Roy asks without breaking a sweat. He runs almost twice as fast as Uncle Roy and barely seems to notice the push-ups. Whatever physical strength and stamina his Raven powers granted him, it's no joke.

When they move on to walking through moves—Colin throwing jabs at the air while Uncle Roy evaluates him—I creep closer to get a better look. Maybe I can learn something, too, and next time we face Kaden, Colin won't have to do it alone.

A hand hauls me back, and I peer up to see Aunt Elaine shaking her head. "Don't get in their way," she warns. "They could hurt you on accident."

The last of my excitement fizzes and dies, and I give up, settling into the grass with Max and my now-cold cup of hot chocolate to watch from the sidelines.

Colin and Uncle Roy break into a sparring match with Aunt Elaine officiating. Uncle Roy's easily three times Colin's size, but he doesn't hold back as much as I expect. When Colin knocks him to the ground with a kick to the ribs hard enough to send up a puff of grass, I understand why: with Colin's powers, he might be even stronger.

A flicker of unexpected jealousy warms my chest as they touch fists for round two. Colin's been magical for all of five seconds, and he's taken to it like a crow to flight. Meanwhile I've lived in a family of psychics my entire life and had my powers for months, and all I'm good at is dodging people in crowded rooms.

"Why did no one ever bother to train *me* this way?" I ask Max as Aunt Elaine corrects Colin's form. We all have different powers, but some are more similar than others: Aunt Elaine's aura reading helped her teach Rose about her empathy, and Gran's telekinesis helped Uncle Roy learn about his pyrokinesis.

My power's similar to Nora's, since we both have visions, but she's never pulled me aside like this. No one has.

Max nudges me with his head, and I scratch behind his ears. "They must think it's not worth it," I tell him. "Why bother? I can't even do anything worthwhile at the inn."

I know I'm sulking, but I can't shake the feeling. Even Aunt Elaine and Uncle Roy, who are only around half the year in total when they're not in Ireland, have important roles here. Uncle Roy handles repairs around the house (of course, he's usually the cause of the damage) and Aunt Elaine coordinates events and is the go-to person for guest services. Rose tends the grounds, Kara handles bookings, and Nora heads it all.

I give people directions.

This is why I have to help stop whatever sinister plan is in motion. I have to prove that my powers are useful. That *I* can be useful and that I belong at Ravenfall.

My determination resurging, I pick up the journal and roll onto my stomach to flick through the pages. If it's full of magical information, maybe it has something about an evil being who can kill with a touch and help wraiths absorb their host's souls.

Max joins me, sometimes batting the page with his paw as it flutters past his face. Whoever did these drawings is really good. Everything is so vivid, and I run my fingers over a sketch of a golem, half expecting to feel it come to life. My dad would love looking through this, if only for all the magical items.

I stop on a drawing of two wicked-looking blades that takes up the whole page. They're smooth and black, with hairline streaks of gold, and I swear they're singing. Max leans an ear to the page; then he starts purring louder than I've ever heard.

Gathering the journal into my arms, I leap to my feet and cross the field to where Colin and Uncle Roy are taking a water break.

"Aunt Elaine," I call, flipping the journal around. "What are these?"

Aunt Elaine gapes at the knives as if they'd jumped out and spooked her, and she takes the journal from me with reverent hands. I haven't seen her this excited since my dad handed over responsibility for Ravenfall's library to her.

"Saint Knives!" Uncle Roy peers wonderingly over his sister's shoulder. "How the heck did they get ahold of a set of those?" He reaches for the journal.

Aunt Elaine sweeps it away. "Bridget, no doubt. But where did she get them?"

"It could have been Niall." Uncle Roy rolls his eyes and mutters, "Acting like you know everything."

Colin stiffens at the mention of his parents' names, and I glower at Aunt Elaine and Uncle Roy, who are too busy bickering to notice. I'm not the only one who could do with being more respectful of other people's emotions. Death is such a normal part of our lives that we barely think of it anymore. Sometimes we forget how real it can be.

"What are they?" I ask again to get them to stop arguing.

The blades, like everything else, look almost alive on the page, the golden streaks glowing brighter than any drawing medium I can think of. What had they done, mixed it with real gold?

I trace the shape with a finger. There's a small triangular chip in the right one, resembling the tip of a cat's ear. They're rendered with such amazing detail that it makes me want to try to re-create the drawing myself.

"Saint Knives are extremely rare," Aunt Elaine explains in her "historian" voice. She and my dad are the readers in the family, though Aunt Elaine loves history in particular, while my dad focuses on magical objects. "They're made from the tombstones of Irish saints who were also members of the Ravenguard, but there were so few of them, and I don't think any remain today. Only the most ancient Irish family lines have them, which—"

"The important thing," Uncle Roy cuts in, "is that they're capable of killing a lot of magical creatures that can't die by other means. Wraiths have other weaknesses, but Saint Knives are extremely effective against them."

That gets Colin's attention. His expression hardens. "How do I use them?"

Aunt Elaine grins mischievously. "That's the fun part." She holds out the journal to him, and Colin takes a deep breath before plunging his hand inside. He withdraws the blades, which glint in the afternoon light.

"Do you have any experience with knives?" she asks, holding out her hand for the blades.

"Some. Liam trained me a little bit." He hands them over, shaking his head. "I can't believe I never figured this out on my own."

Aunt Elaine laughs and holds up the blades. "Saint Knives are the same as any other in regard to wielding them, but they're much lighter than anything you could buy around here. You have to be careful not to forget you're holding them." She flips a knife expertly from her palm to her fingers, catching the blade between her index finger and thumb, a skill I've always envied.

She's taught me a trick or two with throwing knives, but I've never plucked up the courage to try catching them.

"A slash from these will weaken a wraith considerably. A knife to the heart will kill it, but too many smaller wounds will just expel it." Elaine flips the knife back to her palm and holds both up. "Hit them together"—she does, and a pure, melodic sound rings out— "and any wraith nearby will cringe like a dog to a whistle. Weaker ones can be expelled by sound alone."

"Show-off," Uncle Roy mutters.

Aunt Elaine glares at him as she hands Colin the blades. "Let's see what you can do," she says. She disappears into the kitchen and returns a moment later rolling the kitchen table in front of her.

"It's *my* table!" she yells to the house's groans of complaint.

They turn the table on its side, presenting a large round target. Colin's throws aren't terrible, but they aren't great, and Aunt Elaine has to break it down for him a lot more than Uncle Roy did with his hand-to-hand combat instructions. But eventually, he gets the knives to stick point-first into the table.

I let out a congratulatory whistle, and he grins. "Liam only ever taught me to fight with them," he says, pulling the knives free of the table. "Throwing is much harder."

Uncle Roy wipes the sweat from his forehead. "I think that's enough for today. It's getting late. We'll start again first thing tomorrow morning, though."

Colin marvels at the knives in his hands. "One last thing. Do I just knock them together to make them sing?"

Before anyone answers, he slams the blades together, releasing a booming call. The sound sends shivers down my spine, and Max's back arches.

Then Colin collapses.

CHAPTER 13

Colin

Voices echo around me. There's the sound of clanging swords and the pounding of heavy feet.

"For the king!" rings one voice high above the rest. The language isn't English, but I still understand it.

I catch glimpses of green and silver, of people wielding long spears and wooden shields. One person in particular stands out, draped in a forest-green cloak with a swirling symbol and leather armor hemmed in gold autumn leaves. He stops, his sword coated in red, and turns to look at me. His eyes are an unnatural emerald green.

When he sees me, his pupils begin spreading, covering the whites of his eyes and leaving nothing but darkness.

Then it all vanishes, and the real world comes flooding back to me. I gasp; my lungs feel like they're on fire. I try to sit up, but a strong hand pushes me into something soft. I let it, too weak to fight.

My entire body burns, and I feel as if every ounce of energy has been sucked out of me. I just lie there as the colors around me solidify into faces.

Gran leans over me, her brows pinched together. She smiles when she sees I'm awake, a thousand tiny lines spreading from her eyes.

When did she get here?

"There you are," she says.

I try to reply, but my voice comes out in a raspy croak.

"Save your strength," comes an airy voice from my left. A cool cloth presses against my forehead, and I glimpse Rose with a wisp of a smile on her lips.

Anna hovers behind her, one arm wrapped around her stomach, the other hand worrying at her lips. "How is he, Rose?"

"He'll be fine."

I wet my lips and try again. "What happened?" I ask hoarsely.

By now I've worked out we're in the library, but I can't remember how I ended up stretched out across the couch, and the world outside the windows is dark. "The last thing I remember is the Saint Knives."

Anna points at my injured arm. "It was worse than we thought."

I turn my stiff neck to get a glimpse of the scratch, courtesy of Kaden's claws. It looks disgusting. The edges are rimmed in black that reaches out in tiny, vein-like streaks across my chest, shoulder, and ribs. It's as though someone punched me and cracked my skin, and I swear the black spots are pulsing. The dark areas are the only part of my body that feel cold.

I don't have enough energy to panic. Instead, I melt deeper into the couch, feeling overwhelmed. "Kaden did this?"

"It's a wraith toxin," Gran replies. "On a normal human, it'd create hallucinations. But since you're a Raven, your body fought it off for a while. I would surmise the introduction of your new powers, the toxin, and your training were too much to handle all at once."

Something slimy presses against my skin and I flinch, but it's only Rose spreading a light pink paste across the black lines. The burning sensation fades and I close my eyes, sighing in relief.

When I reopen them, a pair of glowing green eyes stares back at me. I recoil before realizing they belong to a very furry, very amused face.

Max.

"He's been waiting to do that." Anna rolls her eyes.

"And here I thought he was worried about me," I mutter. Max curls up behind my head on the pillow, purring softly. The sensation is a tangible lullaby, and my exhaustion soon catches up with me.

Anna chews her lower lip. I can tell she wants to say something, but she's holding the question in.

Rose tilts her head as if catching a distant tune, her eyes fluttering shut. When they reopen, her pale skin is flushed.

"The trees are frightened," she says distantly. "They sense something coming."

"Not the trees again," Anna mutters.

Rose blinks. "I only listen, Anna. I can't control—"

"Yeah, yeah, you can't control what's speaking. But can the trees tell us anything *useful* or are they just going to complain about a bad feeling every time it so much as rains?"

Rose pats her gently on the head. "The trees are the trees."

Exasperation fills Anna's face like steam, but a look from Gran puts an end to their bickering. It's only when they're quiet that I realize I was actually kind of . . . enjoying it? Liam and I would go at it all the time, and I wouldn't talk to him for days after.

I never thought I'd miss arguing with him.

Rose puts the lid on the small clay pot of pink goo. "Apply this twice a day," she instructs me, setting it on the table behind my head.

"And come to me or Rose to change this bandage daily," Gran says, flicking her fingers at a roll of white gauze. It zips over to my arm and begins wrapping it up while Rose holds it aloft. Then it tears itself free and returns to Gran's bag.

"And get some rest tonight," Gran adds sternly. "No training tomorrow."

"But Samhain is only two—" I start, but then stop when Gran frowns. "Yes, ma'am," I say instead. She nods, and she and Rose pack up their things before leaving the room.

Anna drops onto the couch beside me, and the sudden shift in weight makes me roll to the side. I wince as the movement tugs at my arm.

"Sorry," she says.

"How long was I out?" I ask.

Anna casts a worried look out the window. "It's almost midnight. The guests have been complaining about not being able to use the library, but Gran didn't want to move you."

Nearly half a day. The vision had felt like seconds.

"When you, uh, fainted, did you see anything?" she asks.

I blink hazily at her, remembering the odd voice speaking in a language I shouldn't have been able to understand.

"You were muttering," she says. "Aunt Elaine and Uncle Roy didn't hear, but I did. You said, 'For the king!' and then . . ." She shudders, and I'm not sure I want to know the thing that makes Annabella Ballinkay uncomfortable. "The way you screamed, Colin. It scared me."

"I don't really know what I saw," I reply uncertainly. "It was a battle of some sort. But everyone was dressed so strangely, and they were speaking a different language."

Anna's concern deepens. "Wraith toxins can cause hallucinations, but that sounds more like a vision. I couldn't snap you out of it."

I swallow hard. The vision feels like a distant memory now, but in the moment, it felt as real as living it.

"Do you have a pen and paper?" I ask.

Anna springs up, crossing to a long table beside a bookcase and returning with the supplies. I do my best to describe the symbol from the man's cloak in my vision, and she sketches it. It's triangular in shape, formed from three prongs that curve into spirals on the end, giving the impression of constant motion. She adds tiny vines circling around each limb.

"A Triskelion?" she asks.

"You know what it is?"

She nods. "It's a super common Irish symbol, though I've never seen it with the vines. It can mean a lot of different things."

"Can you draw something else for me?" I ask. She listens as I describe the man from my vision. The drawing takes longer than the Triskelion, but by the time she's done, an angular-faced man with a sharp jawline, pointed nose, and large eyes stares up at us, his long hair done in a braid down his neck.

"Who is he?" she asks.

"I don't know. He was wearing a cloak with the symbol." I look around at the library's many books. "Maybe we can do some research tomorrow? See if we can find him or the symbol?"

Anna blanches in response. "Sure, why not. What's another mystery on the list? We can put it right between 'discover evil creature hunting Ravens' and 'where's Liam?'"

I wince at the mention of Liam, and Anna winces along with me. "Sorry," she says. "I'm on edge. I feel like a leaf in a windstorm."

"Try being a leaf in a windstorm who didn't know windstorms existed three days ago," I mutter sleepily.

She smiles faintly. "You're right. I know this hasn't been easy."

Nothing in my life has been for the last few months. This just feels par for the course.

As Anna stands to leave, I finally force out the question I've been holding on to. "Visions . . . they're not normal for a Raven?"

Anna worries her hands in her lap. "No, they're not. It could just be the wraith toxin impacting you differently, though. But until we know, don't tell anyone? If Nora thinks something is wrong, she'll lock us down even more."

I nod in agreement. Nora's just looking for a reason to wrap us in padded suits and hide us in a locked room. What's another inexplicable phenomenon?

"I won't," I tell her.

Anna tries for a reassuring smile and fails as miserably as ever. "Max is going to look after you. Let him or the house know if you need anything."

Once she's gone, I snuggle into the blankets, my exhaustion creeping around me from all sides. I can still hear the echoes of the battle, smell the blood on the air, and no matter how I try, I can't get it out of my head.

It haunts me into my dreams.

Anna brings the twins to the library to help the next day, which I quickly learn is because she absolutely hates reading, and especially research. It's Sunday, which is supposed to be one of their days off from chores too, now that Roy and Elaine are here, so I feel extra guilty asking for help and start to wish I'd just done it all myself.

We tell the twins the truth, since there's no hiding it from Kara, but she promises not to tell Nora so long as we agree to take over feeding Max for a month.

Then we spread out through the library, save Kara, who plops down on the couch with her laptop. Rose, Anna, and I stack books on the tables; everything we can find that might tell us what the Triskelion represents and who the man from my vision is.

Some of the books are ones Elaine already assigned to me to study. Apparently training to become a Raven is a lot more than just perfecting punches and learning how to throw knives. The journal is full of information, but even it isn't all-knowing, so Elaine gave me a list that covers the basics of everything from common supernatural creatures and magical objects to herbology.

As we pore through our respective books, I keep getting caught up reading about how kelpies drown their victims and the dangers of fae deals, before remembering I'm looking for something. It doesn't help that some of the books have magically moving pictures, and others re-create scenes in my head when I touch them.

Magic might have unsettled me when I first discovered it, but now I can't get enough of it. Liam always said I was meant to be a professor or a scientist with the way I consume facts, and surrounded by a magical library, I think that might not be too bad. I want to stay here forever.

No sooner do I have the thought than a fresh wave of guilt comes after. Eventually, Liam is going to find me, and when all this is over, he and I will live together. I can still visit Ravenfall, but it isn't my home, and I owe it to Liam to remember that.

The house brings us mugs of hot chocolate and maple sugar cookies while we work, and Max alternates between lying on our books and knocking our pens off the table. A fire springs up in the hearth to ward off the morning chill, and my energy fades with the cold. I feel a lot better than I did last night, but it's still like someone zapped me dry.

I'm falling asleep in my chair when Kara throws back her head with a groan and says, "There's like a thousand different meanings for that symbol, even without the vines." She balances her laptop on one hand and scrolls down a page with the other. "Spirit, mind, body. That's too easy. Father, son, holy ghost—ha, not that one—past, present, future. That sounds spirit-y. Oooh, this sounds important: creation, preservation, destruction."

"And, of course, the Otherworld, the human world, and the celestial world," Rose adds, pointing to the page she's currently reading. "Also, this book is quite upset about its current placement. I think it'd do better on a shelf with less sunlight."

"Have you found anything about people attached to the symbol in history?" I ask, barely able to see them over the stacks of books around me. Anna gave me a hard time for it, to which I told her there's nothing wrong with being a bibliophile, before having to explain that it means someone who loves books.

"I am *not* a bibliophile," she'd said dryly.

"It doesn't come up as being tied to anyone," says Kara.

I start to say we can't give up, but Kara cuts me off. "Yeah, yeah, nobody was going to give up."

"He's right, though." Anna puts down her pencil from where she'd been doodling in a book. "We don't even have two weeks until Samhain, and who knows what Kaden and his boss are up to in the meantime."

Kara slumps deeper into the couch. "Probably looking for another Raven since they can't reach Colin."

"If he is, he's not having any luck," Rose says as she relocates her book to a dark, dusty shelf. "Nora and Aunt Elaine spent all last night making phone calls. The other Ravens haven't had any wraith encounters, and they didn't know anything about Kaden or his employer."

"No, they aren't coming to help," Kara says before I can ask. "A couple offered, but Nora told them we had it under control. With so many gone already, the Shield is really weak, and she wants to make sure they stay safe."

"Did anyone in town know anything?" Anna asks, but Rose only shakes her head.

"Gran tried a tracking spell on the wraith venom from your wound," Kara says with a nod at my arm. "But it looks as though Kaden got himself warded. That's why we can't find him."

My hands ball into fists. We have so many questions and so few answers. What is Kaden up to right now? Who does he work for, and who was the man in my vision? It feels like we're driving down a narrow road at night without any lights and it's only a matter of time before we crash.

Kara extricates herself from the folds of the couch and resettles her laptop on her knees. "You said the symbol was on a cloak, right?"

The question is more formality, since her fingers are already flying across the keyboard, and I have a feeling she snuck the answer from my head. I go to stand behind her as she opens search boxes and types in words mixed with code. Finally, the screen produces a list of titles. Apparently, someone catalogued the entire library. Probably Elaine. "These are all the books we have on family crests."

The four of us split the list, crowding around my table and flipping through dusty pages with only the occasional sneeze. The house brings us butternut squash soup and chamomile tea, keeping the fire running long into the night, but as the evening drags on, we come up empty.

The twins abandon us after dinner, and Anna gives up not much later, sprawling across her book like it's a pillow. "I'm going to bed," she announces with a face full of paper.

I nod absently.

"I'm telling the house to kick you out if you try to stay in here all night," she warns as she moves toward the door. "Go to bed!"

"Okay," I say, reaching for another book. There has to be an answer here somewhere, and I'm going to find it, even if I have to stay here all night.

CHAPTER 14

Anna

I'm halfway to the stairs when Nora's hushed voice leaks from the kitchen. The door is closed, the soft glow of firelight trickling out underneath it. That alone is enough to make me stop.

We never close the kitchen door. The house doesn't like it.

"Help me out?" I quietly ask the house. The hall floorboards always creak, but the house keeps them quiet for me until I reach the kitchen door.

Leaning close, I put my ear to the brass keyhole, which is just a *little* bigger than normal. I mouth a silent "thank you" to the house as Nora's voice reaches me.

"You aren't listening to me." She sounds frustrated. "If my vision is accurate—"

"Your vision is impossible," Aunt Elaine cuts across her. "You said that battle took place thousands of years ago. How could he have been involved?"

"I don't know! But I saw his face." There's something in Nora's voice that makes me tense.

One of them sets a glass on the table. Then Aunt Elaine says, "I haven't detected anything in his aura, but they've always been hard for me to read. Too much magic. I think you're just worrying too much, Nor."

"That's your answer to everything," Nora snaps. "But what should I expect? You and Roy have always been quick to turn your backs on responsibility when it becomes too much. First Dad, then the inn. Is this to be my responsibility, too, Elaine? Will you be off to Ireland in the morning?"

I flinch. I've never heard Nora talk this way before. Upset, sure, even frustrated, but this? She sounds angry, and beneath that . . . I've never known my mother to be scared.

The silence that follows her words is thick enough to cut. I can only imagine the look Aunt Elaine is giving her, her dark eyebrows furrowed, her lips pursed in what Uncle Roy calls her "unimpressed" face.

I've always known that originally, Aunt Elaine was supposed to take over the inn. Nora had an art scholarship overseas, but then Aunt Elaine got pregnant and followed her fiancé to Ireland. They didn't get married in the end, and her son lives in Dublin with his dad while Aunt Elaine splits her time between them and the inn. And just like that, my aunt ended up the traveler, and my mother the innkeeper.

I never realized how much this bothered Nora before. She does such a great job of running the inn, I thought she'd moved past what happened between her and Aunt Elaine. But even after all these years, the responsibility of Ravenfall weighs on her.

I always thought she wouldn't understand if I told her how I feel, how much it means to me to get things right so I can really be a part of things, but maybe she feels the same pressure.

Finally, Nora sighs. "I'm sorry, El. I just—" She chokes up, and I picture her sister setting a reassuring hand on her shoulder.

"No, I'm sorry," Aunt Elaine says. "You're right. Roy and I haven't been there for you, not how we should. But not this time. Roy and I are going to make sure Colin is prepared. We're going to get through this together, and then the three of us are going to sit down and talk this out."

A moment's silence, then, "All right. But please don't dismiss my concerns. I know he's Bridget's son, but something isn't right. Promise me you'll at least keep an eye on him?"

"Okay."

I draw a sharp breath, loud enough that the kitchen goes quiet. The house masks my retreat as I flee up the steps, already at the second level before the door opens.

Crouched on the stairs, I listen for a sign I've been discovered, but the door swings shut downstairs with a definite *click*.

Still, I don't move, their words replaying in my head.

That battle took place thousands of years ago.

Nora had a vision like Colin's, and for some reason, she thinks something's wrong with him because of it.

My thoughts spin as I return to my room. I barely have the energy to brush my teeth and change, and when I collapse onto my bed, I fall asleep instantly.

I know immediately that I'm dreaming, but I can't make myself wake up. It's like being trapped inside a vision; everything feels real.

I'm standing at the edge of the wood outside the house, still in my pajamas, my bare toes curling into the grass and soil. The Shield spreads out before me in a line, disappearing into the black sky above.

Silence fills the night, the kind of quiet that promises something big to come.

There's no wind, no rain, no rustling of leaves. Even the house is silent, its windows darker than I've ever seen.

I reach out to touch the Shield. The movement is both my own and not. I'm somehow myself and some outside presence floating above, watching. My fingers brush the barrier; it's cold, so cold it zaps the heat from inside me.

It cracks beneath my touch. I recoil, my heart drumming against my chest. Movement to my side makes me turn, and I come face to face with Colin, a smile on his face. It looks wrong.

"Colin." My breath comes out as mist. Suddenly I realize how dark it is. There are no stars, no moon. The only light comes from the glow of the Shield, and it's waning quickly. The world is upside down, similar to the in-between I glimpse when I travel through the big oak tree.

"You should have known better," Colin says quietly. It sounds nothing like him. His voice is low, nearly a growl. "How ignorant you all are."

I want to step away from him, but my body won't move. The part of me watching from above screams at myself to run, but my voice doesn't reach. The light from the Shield is nearly gone now, and as the last of it fades away, Colin begins to laugh.

The brightness of his silver eyes is all I can see. But as his laughter rises, his pupils expand, the darkness overtaking his eyes until there's nothing left.

Then the Shield shatters.

An inhuman wail pierces the night. I slam my hands over my ears, but it cuts through them, barreling into my head, into my body, into my soul. It fills me up, sucking every inch of warmth from inside me.

Faces swirl around me. Decomposing, skinless faces in different states of decay, trailed by white auras draped in shadows. The spirits flood out, shrieking like banshees. And underneath it all, I can hear Colin laughing.

When I wake, I'm sitting up. The cold has followed me from the dream and my skin crawls. Something light but solid sits in my lap, my fingers curled around an object. Slowly, I force myself to look.

A small sketch pad sits in my lap, a pencil in my hand. The side of my fingers and palm are covered in graphite, the muscles cramped. Drawn on a page in the middle of my sketchbook is a basic replica of the scene from my dream.

I flip back a page. I've drawn the same scene moments earlier than the next page. I flip back another, and another, each one showing the scene a little earlier. Slamming the notebook shut, I place my thumb on the edge of the pages and flip rapidly through them. The pictures seem to move, bringing the scene to life until I reach the final page.

On it, the spirits churn around me, and Colin's eyes are black as night.

With the Samhain party approaching, there's more to do than ever around the house, and business is steadily creeping up. Nora, Aunt Elaine, and the twins are booked for psychic readings almost every day. Uncle Roy does fire shows in the evenings, hitting far-off targets and making ribbons of flame dance. Even the house is feeling the need to outdo itself, rattling windows and creaking floorboards in the dead of night. It even has Max changing its hat twice a day.

Meanwhile, I pick the moonflowers out of the garden to prevent guests from falling under their enchantments, string rowanberries together as party favors, and capture wisps to let loose come the big night.

I barely get a moment to myself, and I've started to suspect it's all because of Nora. She wants to keep me busy instead of focusing on how little progress we've made with Kaden and his mysterious employer. Nora put the town on alert for signs of wraiths, but so far no one's reported anything, and Rose's girlfriend, Dilara, came out with another witch from the cottages to check on Ravenfall's wards. But other than that, it's been quiet. Almost too quiet, like the calm before the storm.

At first, I'm okay with it. Staying busy keeps me from worrying about Nora's conversation with Aunt Elaine, or the strange dream of Colin I had that I'm starting to worry might have been some sort of vision.

There are lots of different types of vision powers. Some people get premonitions, enabling them to see the future; others have recognition and can see the past. I see death, and Nora sees both the future and past. But all of us, no matter our specific powers, sometimes get visions of other kinds, usually when really powerful magic is involved.

That thought only scares me more, and I throw myself into my tasks. But after three days of it, I can't take another chore.

More than once I escape outside to watch Colin train with Aunt Elaine and Uncle Roy, but it only makes me itch to do something more useful than chores. So much so that I even help Colin keep researching the symbol and man from his vision, though we've yet to make any progress.

Right now, he's sparring with Uncle Roy in the morning mist, the sunlight glancing off the Saint Knives in bright orange beams.

He's already gotten better with them, and I have to squash another flicker of jealousy. He took to his new powers like a sprite to a flame, whereas I can barely handle mine. Colin's been a Raven all of a few days and he's already being useful.

I'm scrubbing faerie dust off the deck.

The scent of pumpkin spice trickles out of the kitchen, and I hear Kara's and Rose's laughter a moment later. Tossing my rag into a nearby bucket, I dash inside, where a pumpkin hot chocolate waits for me in a chipped blue mug on the table.

My sisters are already sitting there, their feet propped on each other's laps, cheeks rosy from their warm drinks. Kara's on her phone, holding a one-sided conversation with Rose while she sorts different-colored petals from a basket on the table.

"What about flowers?" Kara says to Rose's unspoken thought. "Dilara loves flowers." Pause. "Yes, I know she works at a flower shop." Pause. "I am not bad at giving gifts!"

I sit down, pulling my hot chocolate close. There's a cinnamon maple leaf drawn on top of the whipped cream, and I take a deep breath of the spiced scent. The house makes the best drinks.

Rose hands me a yellow rose petal. "Yellow is not your color," she says as if I'm supposed to know what that means. I'm mostly used to Rose's distracted ways, but sometimes I wish she came with a manual.

"Neither is pink," Kara says with a smirk. "You have faerie dust on your nose."

"You have a pimple on yours," I shoot back. "Oh wait, that's just your nose."

Kara's hand pauses halfway to her face and she glowers at me. "Fine. I guess I won't tell you our news, then."

I perk up. "What news?"

She twirls a few strands of long hair around her finger. "The thing is, Dilara wants to take us out tonight—"

"—for ice cream!—" Rose interjects excitedly.

"—but Rose is supposed to pull the bluebells out of the garden, and I need to schedule readings for Aunt Elaine for the next couple days, so we just won't have time to tell you beforehand." Kara makes an exaggerated show of standing.

I groan. "Fine. I'll do your chores. Just tell me!"

She drops into her chair and pulls a folded paper out of her pocket. "Nora's network finally turned up a lead." She smooths the paper out on the table, revealing a photo shot from a security camera of Kaden with two people. The first is a white man with black hair I don't recognize; the other is a woman who seems familiar, but I can only see a sliver of her light brown face. The glint of one silver eye creates a halo across the rest.

"Kaden has two new wraith friends," Kara says grimly. "I guess now we know what he's been up to while he can't get to Colin."

My stomach drops at the sight of the photo. This must be why Kaden has been lying low: he's recruiting more wraiths. We could barely handle one. What are we going to do against three?

Rose pats my shoulder consolingly, leaving a petal behind on my shirt. "Don't worry. Colin is safe with the trees."

Safe, but no closer to discovering who the wraiths are working for and what he wants, and Samhain is just over a week away. Whatever they're up to, it's going down soon.

"Does Nora know about this?" I ask.

Kara nods. "She's trying to track down who they are and see if they're from Wick. If they are, she thinks Kaden's been sticking around town."

I raise my mug and mutter behind it, "Meanwhile, you two are going out for ice cream."

Kara rolls her eyes. "You're just in a bad mood because Colin's the golden child and you're still swapping out glamour bags."

I nearly choke on my hot chocolate. My unhappiness with my chore-filled life the last few months hasn't been a secret, but the twins haven't acknowledged it before.

"Kara," Rose chides softly, but Kara doesn't relent.

"Maybe he should take your place at the inn," Kara continues. "At least he's not scared of his powers."

"I'm not scared!"

Kara's voice turns mocking. "'It was terrible, Nora. I can't get their faces out of my head. Why are my powers so useless?'" She throws a dramatic hand across her forehead, then smirks at me. "Don't forget, sis, I hear everything."

It's all I can do not to throw my steaming hot chocolate in her face. Instead, I wipe my fisted hand across my nose and blow the sparkling faerie dust into her face. "Sneezes," I command.

"Ah-choo! Anna! Ah-choo! I'm going—*ah-choo!*—to kill you!"

But I've already bolted from the kitchen and up the wrought-iron staircase on the side of the house to the rooftop garden. The stairs empty into a widow's walk, and I dive randomly down one of the black stone paths, disappearing into a cloud of brightly colored flowers.

Eventually I slow along a curtain of ivy, the sound of rushing water rustling behind it. Wind chimes jingle softly in the wind, sounding as forlorn as I feel. I follow the curving path into an alcove of plants and drop onto the stone bench beside the pond, feeling as though I might cry.

Kara's always been a bit of a jerk, but in this case, she's right. My powers *are* useless, I *am* scared of them, and as much as I don't want it to be true, I even feel a little jealous of Colin.

Okay, a lot jealous.

All my life I've wanted what he practically tripped and fell into, and I'm starting to think, no matter what I do, I'll never get it. Not with Colin and his magic overshadowing everything, not with my entire family involved now.

What do they need my powers for? What can I do that the rest of them can't?

Kara's right: Colin belongs here more than I ever will.

The plants whisper, sliding closer together and sealing off the alcove. A moment later I hear the crunch of gravel, and Colin's worried voice calling, "Anna? Anna, are you up here?"

"It's okay," I tell the house. "He can come in."

The flowers retreat, revealing the opening to the alcove just as Colin curves around the path. The smile on his face only makes me feel guilty.

"There you are." He joins me on the bench. "I'm pretty sure the house was taking me in circles. I'm starting to think it doesn't like me"

"It thinks you're friends with Max," I grumble.

"Is that bad?"

"There is no greater offense in this world or the next."

Colin actually looks worried, so I tack on a smile, but there's really no telling whether the house will get past its grudge. It's always liked me, so it doesn't care that Max and I get along, too, but it's never been known to be a forgiving structure.

"Are you okay?" Colin asks, making me realize I've been smiling awkwardly at a rosebush for the last minute.

My reflex is to say yes, but he's looking at me with such an open, earnest expression that it would feel like lying. Because I'm not okay.

"I'm useless." I play with the strings on my sweatshirt. "Everyone else in my family can use their power to do something for the inn, and I can't."

It sounds petty saying it out loud, and I go back to staring at the bush. He'll probably tell me it doesn't matter, that I'm overreacting. Everyone else does. But as I look up at him, he faces me and waits. Listening.

Drawing a deep breath, I say, "This inn is my life. It's all our lives. I grew up here, I worked here, I learned here. Ravenfall's my favorite place in the world, but it's . . ." I trail off, clenching my jaw. What am I doing? He doesn't care.

I can't stop myself from trying to make friends. When I was younger, I used to try to befriend the kids who traveled with their families. But they never wanted to hang out with the weird girl at the inn. The guests come, get what they need from us, and then return to their lives.

It's the only part of living at Ravenfall I've never gotten used to—for me, this place is my life, and everyone else leaves eventually.

Even Colin will leave, once Liam returns.

"It's what?" he asks gently, surprising me.

"I just don't know that I belong here," I tell him, and it isn't until I say it that I realize that's my real fear. I didn't fit in at school and my dad didn't want me on his expeditions with him. If I don't belong at Ravenfall, then do I belong anywhere?

Colin laughs. I stare at him, embarrassed, but he says quickly, "I'm sorry. It's just—I can't imagine you anywhere but Ravenfall," he says. "There's so much more to you than your magic. You've taught me so much, and you made me feel comfortable in an entirely new world. And you're risking yourself to help me find out

127

who killed my parents. You're brave, and smart, and good at figuring stuff out, and I couldn't ask for a better partner."

He offers me a smile. "Psychometry isn't your only power, Anna. And you're not useless."

I swallow hard. It feels good to hear someone say those things, especially someone not from my family, who are too close to understand. They all matter to the inn—they can't see what it's like to feel like I don't.

In the end, I settle for a smile. "Thanks. You're not half bad yourself. Aunt Elaine and Uncle Roy are pretty impressed with you."

"They're good teachers," he says, rubbing the back of his head. "Though they argue a lot."

"Siblings," I say with a wave, and watch his face shutter. I consider throwing myself over the roof's edge. "Sorry," I say with a wince.

He smiles easily and stands. "It's nothing. Come on, dinner's ready."

I follow him, feeling much better, but also resolved. He's right—I do have more to offer than just my powers.

And I know just how to prove it.

CHAPTER 15

Colin

Anna and I talk all dinner. She tells me about all the different times Roy broke parts of the house or scorched it with his pyrokinesis, and how the house would make the walls in his room creak and the floor shake until he got up and fixed them. I tell her about Liam's addiction to reality television and list the army of pop culture facts taking up residence in my brain.

I barely even notice the time passing the next few days. I train and help Anna with her chores, getting to know her family as we prepare for Samhain. The air grows crisper, the lawn blanketed with crunchy golden leaves. Wisps dance through the trees and crows gather in the grass and on the branches, scattering with angry caws when Max goes bounding through them.

We drink hot apple cider and sit wrapped in knitted blankets in the library as Roy regales us with stories from Ireland. He talks about how he met his husband—who runs a farm in Ireland and is planning to visit for Samhain—and tells us stories from how they both got lost in a castle ruin to the time he nearly followed a kelpie into the sea.

And through it all, Liam's absence is a physical presence.

I've spent a few mornings sitting alone in the Charger, breathing in the familiar scent of the old pine air freshener. Though the car belonged to my mom, it's Liam I associate most with it. He was always outside fixing it up, washing it, detailing it. Whenever we had an errand to run, Liam would volunteer, just so he could drive it.

Some of my best memories are driving in that car with him, like the time we escaped our latest motel to drive through a big redwood forest on the California coast. We parked up in the mountains and hiked all day, and Liam bought me ice cream on the way home. When we got back, Mom and Dad were furious at him. They shut the door so I couldn't hear, but I remember Liam's voice to this day.

"He needs to do something normal once in a while!"

"Pay attention!" Elaine barks at me during training that morning. "We don't have time for you to daydream, Colin. Samhain is only a few days away."

I flinch, having been distracted by the house's wide-brimmed hat, the edges decorated in orange and gold flowers. It's the kind someone would wear to a horse race or a tennis match.

It's Saturday, and Anna lies in the grass by the sloping hill, resketching the same drawing of a pocket dragon she's been practicing for the last few days. She looks so relaxed, and I envy her a bit. I'm exhausted.

"Oh, cut him a break, El," Roy says. "We've been at it for hours."

"He needs to be ready," Elaine returns sharply. "We don't know what we'll face on Samhain, or when the wraiths will make their next move."

Nora had expanded her network to a couple other local towns, but shortly after they had confirmed the second man in Kara's photo was from Wick, too, which meant Kaden was probably sticking around town. Some of the local witches had volunteered to search Hollowthorn Woods, since no one had seen Kaden in town, but the woods were too vast to check everywhere. The other theory was that they were staying at the home of the third wraith's host body, who they hadn't been able to identify yet, probably preparing to gather more wraiths.

Roy flips a tiny flame between his fingers like a coin. "He's already taken a wraith on once. And you know what they say: what doesn't kill you—"

"Usually tries again," Elaine says grimly.

It sobers Roy right up, and he returns the Saint Knives to me from the target.

Loosening my wrists, I feel the weight of the knives and gauge the distance to the scarred kitchen table. It's about ten feet away. Not a huge distance, but about as far as the Saint Knives can really be thrown. They're too large and light to go much farther, made instead for close combat.

I hit the center with both knives.

I've been struggling with throwing the knives the last few days, so it feels good to finally get it right. The hand-to-hand fighting is definitely my strength, thanks to the few months I spent training with Liam. Plus, my enhanced strength and speed and improved senses make it all a lot easier.

Elaine retrieves the knives, but she doesn't give them to me. "I want to work on a new skill today," she says. "Knives can be great long-range weapons, but they're one-time use for most people. Ravens, on the other hand, are capable of materialization."

"Cause to appear?" I ask, thinking of the definition of *materialize*.

She nods. "It's an important skill for Ravens, since carrying a journal around isn't exactly convenient. You need to know how to summon things from afar."

Excitement flutters through me at the idea. Every day I spend training opens up new possibilities for my powers, and I've been throwing myself into learning, spending hours in the library reading. Not just about Ravens, but about psychics and supernatural creatures and all types of magic. I've learned more words the last few days than ever.

"How do I do it?" I ask.

"It's not much different than the way you pull items from the pages already." Elaine holds the knives out in her palms. "Focus on the size and shape of the item, how it would feel to hold it, and imagine yourself pulling it from my hands."

The technique isn't as simple as it sounds. I try to focus on the things Elaine said, but my thoughts drift. First to the knives, then to the strange vision I had, then to Kaden. Nothing happens.

Elaine is unimpressed. "Focus."

I try again, but the knives still don't move.

Elaine purses her lips thoughtfully. "When I read someone's aura, it helps me to imagine it as a shape and color. Otherwise I just get vague impressions and feelings. But when I give the thought a tangible connection, everything gets clearer."

A flame sparks to life in Roy's palm. "My pyrokinesis is the same way. I have to think of the flame as a part of myself to be able to control it."

A tangible connection. A part of myself. I repeat the words over and over again as I focus on the knives. I think about the way the edges curve, about the touch of cool metal in my hands. My fingers curl in, mimicking their size, the grip. I imagine picking the blades up out of her hands, of them becoming a part of me.

The knives shiver, then disappear, reappearing clasped in my hands. Their cool touch startles me, and I nearly drop them.

"I'm not sure I'll ever get used to all of this," I say reverently.

"You don't have to get used to it," Roy says with a grin. "You just have to get good at it."

"In three days," I mutter. What if I haven't learned enough to defend myself against Kaden and his boss?

Roy claps my shoulder, nearly knocking me forward despite my new strength. "You're doing great, kid." He offers me a smile. "And you're not alone in this."

Guilt makes my stomach twinge. "I'm sorry." I dragged them all into this, and now they have no choice but to be involved. "Involving you wasn't fair. You should leave me and Kaden to each other."

Roy's laugh is practically a bark, so loud and abrupt that I jerk my head up in surprise. Beside him, Elaine looks offended. "Family doesn't only mean blood around here, Colin," he says, nodding at something over my shoulder.

Anna is moving toward us, her sketchbook tucked under her arm. The late autumn sunlight filters through the burnt-orange leaves at her back, Max pouncing on bugs in the grass ahead of her. "It doesn't even always mean human."

My stomach twists again as Max bounds over. He leaps, and on instinct I stick out an arm. He lands on my forearm with control beyond that of a cat and clambers up to perch on my shoulders.

When my parents died and Liam didn't show, I started to feel really alone. I suddenly realize how much that has been affecting me, and my rising emotions threaten to come spilling out. I hold my breath, prepared to let the burn distract me, but then Anna stops before us and says to Max, "Fine. You win."

Out of the corner of my eye, I see Max bow.

The ridiculousness of the action isn't what gets me. It's how natural the absurdity feels.

"Do I want to know?" I ask.

Anna grins. "I bet Max that if he leapt at you again, you'd still freak out. Guess I was wrong."

"And his prize?" Elaine asks.

Anna folds her arms. "I have to be a black cat at the party."

I laugh, and it's like a dam breaking open, it feels so good. Anna shoots me a dark look. "Speaking of which, you need a costume."

My laughter dies. "I am not dressing up." I fold my arms in defiance, but Anna only looks more determined.

"Everyone dresses up."

I groan, and Roy laughs. "Go get cleaned up," he says. "Tonight's bonfire night!"

I shower before meeting Anna at her room. Her sweater tonight says TEA REX above the dinosaur clasping a teacup in its short arms. We've just stepped onto the deck when Kara pulls us aside, a roll of papers clasped in her hand. "I think I finally tracked down our symbol in a book from Gran's collection," she says, unfurling the papers.

We all peer down at the top paper, which is full of text and a large image of a Triskelion, the spirals wrapped in thorny vines. "It's the family crest of Fin Varra."

"Who?" I ask.

Kara turns the paper toward him. "Most of what I could find is in Irish. There was very little on the internet about him. Apparently, he was the king of the Tuatha Dé Danann, or the faerie folk. But he also had another name." The look she gives me makes my stomach swoop.

"The King of the Dead."

A slow, uneasy feeling unfurls in my stomach, and I exchange worried looks with Anna.

"King of the Dead?" I repeat. "As in the devil?"

Kara shakes her head. "Totally different idea. He's more of an Irish god, if anything." She shifts to the next paper. "The story goes he and his people, the Tuatha, were driven underground by another group in Ireland. What's weird is some of the sources say underground, and some say another realm."

She shrugs, lowering the papers. "The internet's not super reliable on this, and all I could find in the library was in Irish. I was going to ask Gran about it, but she was in such a rush to head out tonight that she didn't stop to listen. She was shutting me out of her mind, too, which is rude."

"But why did Colin have a vision of him?" Anna asks.

"That," Kara says, "is above my pay grade. Now come on, I want s'mores."

We follow her to a paved circle off the corner of the house. A dome-shaped fire pit sits on each of several stone platforms, surrounded by chairs filled with guests drinking Wish Cider and hot chocolate in the glow of the firelight. Roy is busy building a pyre in one, surrounded by the other Ballinkays.

Nora and Elaine clutch cups of hot spiced cider, and Rose is setting up ingredients for s'mores. Anna descends on a chair, and I collapse into one beside her as flames soar from Roy's hands, setting the wood ablaze. My muscles are putty, and I happily allow the chair to support every ounce of my weight. Despite the cool night air and the still-building fire, my skin feels hot and sweaty, and all I can think about is Kara's revelation. It feels like for every answer we get, a hundred more pop up.

Kaden is lying low gathering more wraiths, but what is he planning to do with them? The man in my vision was an ancient Irish god, but what does he have to do with me, and how am I even having a vision of him?

Anna pokes me with a stick, breaking my thoughts. She offers it to me with a marshmallow and a look that says, *Marshmallows now, panic later.*

"What am I supposed to do with these?" I ask.

Her eyes widen. It takes her a moment, but she finally realizes I'm kidding. A smile breaks across her face and she laughs.

"And here I thought you didn't know what a joke was," she says, sticking a marshmallow on the end of her stick.

I smirk, copying her, and set it to roast over the flames. "I've learned a thing or two since coming here."

Roy pours the hot cider into mugs and hands them around. We make s'mores, talk, and drink, the cool night warmed by the flames. At some point, Max shows up and curls up in my lap, fast asleep, his paws resting on the journal that's sticking out of my pocket.

"Can I borrow this?" Anna taps the journal. "For, uh, a surprise."

My gut instinct is to say no. It's one of the last things I have of my parents. But I trust Anna and know she'll take good care of it.

"Sure. Just drop it by my room when you're done with it." I hand it to her, and she settles it in her lap.

Someone pulls out a pack of cards, and we all start playing poker. I picked up the rules from Liam, who would play to make extra cash on the side. Kara promises not to use her powers, but her eagle eyes are so keen I feel like they see into my very soul. It's Anna's turn to deal, and as the game goes on, I begin to watch her carefully. Finally, she stops and meets my gaze.

"Are you dealing from the bottom?" I ask suspiciously.

She freezes. "I would never." She holds my gaze as she very slowly, very purposefully, deals the next card from the top of the deck.

I roll my eyes, and she laughs. "Where'd you even learn that?" she asks.

I snatch the deck from her, not doubting for a second she'll do it again if I look away. "Liam used to play sometimes, and he'd take me along."

"Mountebank," Anna accuses, and I stare at her in surprise. She grins. "You're not the only one who knows fancy words. It means a person who tricks others for money!"

Nora swats Roy. "I told you to stop teaching her these things."

He holds up his hands innocently. "I would never."

"Straight," Rose says simply. "For once."

"Straight flush." Kara drops her cards atop her sister's with a flourish. She or Rose have won every game we've played.

Anna gestures at them. "That's why I learned."

I laugh, and in that moment, I feel like a puzzle piece finally slotted into place. Is this what my life would have been if my parents had never left Wick? Had they once sat where I sit now, eating s'mores and playing cards? Mom would have been so competitive, then grumpy whenever she lost, and Dad would have cajoled her into trying again. He'd have been the first asleep, and Mom the last to leave.

I try to picture them there, and I hold on to that image as I gather up the cards to deal again, content to drink apple cider and play cards by the fire forever.

CHAPTER 16

Anna

I splay Colin's journal out before me on my bed that night, my hair still smelling faintly of bonfire smoke and my stomach full of s'mores and cider. I've been practicing drawing a mechanical pocket dragon for days, ever since our talk in the garden. Eventually Colin will want to add something to the journal, and the first step is drawing an image, one of the few skills he actually doesn't have.

If my psychometry powers aren't going to come in handy with Kaden, maybe I can be useful another way, and what better way to do that than with something I *know* I'm good at? I've been drawing for as long as I can remember, and the least I can do is help Colin out after he listened to me in the garden.

I've just touched the pencil to the paper when the journal leaps into the air. It shudders once, then snaps shut before falling to the bed.

Startled, I reach out a tentative finger to flip open the cover. It doesn't budge. Cold panic bubbles up inside me and I grab both edges, trying to force it open. A shock buzzes against my skin, and I drop the journal with a yelp.

It's no good. It's locked down.

"No, no, no, no," I groan. "What is wrong with you?"

The book remains resolutely silent, and my panic redoubles. What do I do? I can't return it to Colin like this, and I can't go to someone for help. Nora doesn't need another reason to keep me on the sidelines, and the last thing I want is to be responsible for interrupting Colin's training with so little time left before Samhain.

"It'll probably be fine in the morning," I tell myself, sticking the journal under my pillow. But as I snuggle under the covers, my stomach only twists tighter.

It is *not* fine in the morning.

The journal still won't open, so I default to plan B and return it to Colin while rushing him to get ready. Last night we convinced Nora to let Rose take us to the costume shop to pick out our outfits for the party. Since Colin is warded, the wraiths won't be able to track him, and we have Max as an extra precaution. Still, we promise to be careful.

As I hoped, Colin tosses the journal onto the bed and joins me in the hall without trying to open it. Now that he can materialize, he doesn't need to bring it with him.

"Come straight home!" Nora calls as Colin and I disappear out the front door with Max in tow.

Rose drives and I sit up front, flipping through music channels as we go. Colin sits middle back, with Max lounging across his shoulders, his tail curled around his neck. We have the windows down despite the cold and leave them even when it starts to drizzle, the fresh scent of pine trees filling the air.

"Is this party a masquerade or a costume ball?" Colin asks as we pull up outside the costume shop. It's a hole-in-the-wall made of dark stone, with an entryway so crowded by costumes and Halloween decorations that it's a miracle anyone ever goes inside.

THE FINAL MASQUERADE is scrawled across the glass window with flaking crimson paint.

Everyone in Wick gets their costumes here. They always have the weirdest and most unique stuff, some of it woven with a little magic. The problem is that the store is a lot like a costume trunk at a kid's party: you never know what you're going to find, and it might not always be complete.

"Both," I reply as I clamber out of the car to join him. "It started out as a masquerade, because all that matters on Samhain is that your face is hidden to ward off the evil spirits. But when we started drawing a bunch of tourists, my family opened it up to costumes, too, since most Americans celebrate Halloween, not Samhain."

"So I can just get a mask, then?" Colin says hopefully. Max is still balanced effortlessly on his shoulders, and Colin hardly seems to notice, as if the cat has been there all his life.

I feign a pout. "I have to go as a black cat—*the* most cliché costume ever—and you get away with a mask? I don't think so."

I stare him down, but when Max uses my own tactic against me, blinking his big round eyes with as much adorableness as he can muster, I break.

"Don't you help him out of this!" I say. He sticks his tongue out at me and I'm forced to turn around to hide my laughter. "Come on, Rose is already inside."

A bell rings overhead when we enter. The shop is narrow but deep, and every inch is as cluttered as the front. Rose is nowhere to be seen, already hidden behind the layers of clothing and masks. This won't be the first time I've had to track her down in a store.

Colin stands rigid by the front door, his arms crossed, making a point not to look at anything. I hold up a feathery blue mask with tiny crystals embedded in it. "You can pick out your costume, or I can," I tell him with a grin.

He lets out an overly dramatic sigh and starts inspecting the costumes. He returns a few minutes later with a very fake-looking suit stained with even faker blood.

I raise an eyebrow. "What's that supposed to be?"

"A mortician."

I eye his all-black clothing. "You don't need a costume for that."

One corner of his lips twitches, as if he's fighting a smile, and he disappears into the clutter again. While he's gone, I find a long black tail that I can pin onto the back of my pants. Now all I need is a mask.

I collect a couple of costumes for Colin to try on, though I don't really expect him to. To my delight, he accepts them grudgingly and disappears into the changing room. I sit down in a chair outside, Max resting on the arm of it.

A moment later he reappears dressed in a headless horseman outfit, his plastic pumpkin head under an arm. The costume is at least two sizes too small, the arms and legs falling several inches short and the shoulders bursting at the seams. His trinity knot tattoo pokes out the top.

"I don't think you have that on right," I say. Max shakes his head.

"What do you mean?" He looks down at the black felt. "I don't see how I could wear it any differently."

I stifle a grin. Colin frowns and faces a nearby mirror, seeing for the first time how funny the costume looks. His expression is the last straw. My laughter fills the shop, and beside me, Max shakes with amusement.

Muttering to himself, Colin disappears back into the dressing room. I hear a distinct tear and exchange glances with Max. When Colin reappears, I hold up a beautiful black and gold masquerade mask. "Maybe you should just go with this?" I suggest.

It takes him a moment to realize I never meant to force him to wear a real costume to begin with, but when he does, he snatches the mask out of my hand and tosses the headless horseman costume onto a pile of tutus with such ferocity I half expect it to burst into flame.

I giggle but stop when I realize what's sitting beside the multicolored pile of fluff. It's a black cat mask, and it's beautiful. It's not your run-of-the-mill felt cutout, but rather handmade from a solid black ceramic. Once upon a time it was probably very expensive.

I snatch it and turn to the mirror, fixing the mask on my face. It looks so realistically catlike. The mask is hard and sticks out from my face a little bit to actually form the cat's maw. Delicate silver designs trace the edges of the ears and eyes, but the best part is the forehead. Sticking out of it are two long, hornlike prongs, with two shorter ones beside them.

Whoever made this mask knew a Jabberwocky.

"What do you think?" I turn toward Colin and everything shifts, becoming hazy and tinged with magic.

Colin is gone, and in his place stands a man with hair dark as night and eyes greener than the hills behind him. He steps toward me, two black and gold knives in his hands, his muscled body clad in molded leather. He speaks, but the words are in Irish. A shield covers half his body, a three-legged spiral painted across it encased in winding thorny vines.

The Triskelion.

Slowly, his eyes turn completely black.

Then Rose appears in front of him, giant white wings sprouting from her back—an angel costume. The vision dissolves as she slips the mask off my face, her expression uncharacteristically worried. An even more troubled Colin hovers over her shoulder.

"Did you see that?" I ask.

She tilts her head, listening to something I can't hear. "You had a vision. No, I didn't see it. Also, someone followed us."

"What do you mean?" Colin scans the shop. "The place is empty."

A low rumbling fills the room as Max presses low to the ground. The edges of his fur begin to flicker between solidity and translucence, a sure sign that he's sensing bad magic.

Rose peers down at him as if she's seeing him for the first time. "Don't you think it's strange that Seamus hasn't come to greet us?"

"Yeah, I guess it is," I say absently, studying the mask in my hand. I'm no stranger to magical objects, and I've never heard of a mask that gives its wearer visions, but that much I can take. What's got me fighting a shiver is that I'm pretty sure I just saw the same man Colin did in his vision, and I only saw him when I looked *at Colin.*

Plus, his eyes turned black, same as Colin's in my dream. And there's something else, too, something about those knives that I can't get out of my head. . . .

"I found him unconscious in his office," Rose replies.

My head snaps up and I groan. "You should have led with that. Can you sense which way whoever followed us is? We can escape out the opposite door."

Rose shakes her head. "I feel them everywhere."

"How—" I start to ask, but stop when something moves by the wall. A grim reaper costume unhooks itself and lands on its feet. Its movements are stiff and jerky as it lifts its head, bone fingers curling around the shaft of its scythe.

It slashes for me and I throw my arms up reflexively. The blade slices along my forearm, and I stare in horror as blood wells from the cut.

"It's real," I whisper.

The grim reaper is no longer a costume, but flesh and blood, with a gleaming metal scythe.

And it does not look happy.

CHAPTER 17

Colin

My heart stops as the reaper lunges for Anna again. I catch the shaft of the scythe on the downstroke and we struggle for control of the weapon. I twist around, putting my back into its chest and heaving. It flies over my head, slamming hard into the ground where Anna, Rose, and Max were a moment ago.

Except they're gone.

I start to call out for them when the reaper's foot connects with my stomach, knocking the wind out of me. I throw my shoulder into its arm, and the scythe clatters to the ground. Still struggling for breath, I dive for it, seizing the shaft and turning as the reaper lunges for me. It drives its chest straight into the curved blade.

I brace for the spray of blood, but it doesn't come. Its weight vanishes as the solidness of the reaper disappears, leaving me blanketed in black cloth. I throw it off, and the now-fake scythe rolls to the ground with a harmless clatter of plastic.

Then a pair of arms seize me from behind, lifting me off the ground. I glimpse fur before I'm hurled into a wall of costumes, sending masks and capes scattering. I scramble to my feet in time to dodge a punch from a werewolf that drives a hole in the wall.

Taking a few short breaths to calm myself down, I focus on the feel of my Saint Knives in my hands—cold, metallic, light.

Nothing happens.

The link between me and the journal feels cold and inaccessible. I try again, but it doesn't so much as quiver.

Then the werewolf is on me.

It grabs me by the shirt and lifts me with ease. Claws dig sharply into my collarbone, its breath hot and sour on my face.

I drive my fist into its snout hard enough to crunch bone—and it collapses into a pile of brown clothes.

"Colin!" Anna's voice rings out from across the shop. I run toward it, following a silver glow rebounding off the wall, and emerge by the cash register.

Anna and Rose have a dark-haired woman trapped against the wall. She looks familiar, but I can't place her. Max sits on Anna's shoulder, his whole body glowing silver. Anna clutches her wounded arm to her chest, a cloth pressed against it.

"She's the third wraith from Kara's photo with Kaden," Anna says.

"You're possessing a witch," Rose says wonderingly. "How?"

That's why she looks familiar! It's the witch from the bakery, the one who gave me and Anna cream puffs that tasted like sunshine.

The wraith bares her teeth.

"You can either tell us what we want to know, or I can let Max absorb your spirit." Anna places her uninjured hand on Max's head. He leans into it, his eyes gleaming malevolently.

Fear flickers through the wraith's expression. "Her magic is weak. Her wards were easy to overcome to take her body."

I look from her to Max. "You're afraid of Max. Which means you haven't absorbed your host's soul like Kaden did. You can be expelled."

The wraith sneers. "I'm not strong enough to do it myself, but my lord will make me a permanent resident when he returns. He'll make us all permanent, and then the living will belong to the dead!"

Anna's face lights up. "So we're right: whoever you're working for *does* have the power to help you absorb your host's souls!"

"He has power over more than that, psychic. You know not what you stand against."

"How did you find us?" I edge closer.

"Why, thanks to you, of course, little Raven," the wraith says with a wide grin.

I recoil, exchanging confused looks with Anna. "What?"

"You led us straight here."

"You're lying. That's not possible; he's warded." Anna's voice shakes, and she looks to Rose, whose freckled face is nearly white. But the wraith only laughs a high, howling sound, her whole body shaking with it.

"Colin," Rose says. "Your knives."

"I . . . I can't summon them," I say apologetically. "Something's wrong with my connection to the journal."

Anna's face pales, and the wraith laughs again. "Having trouble, little Raven?"

I round on her. "Tell us who you work for!"

The wraith's black eyes grow wide as gaping maws. "You're all dead," she hisses, and lunges for Anna.

Max leaps from Anna's shoulder with a roar, transforming midair. His translucent body passes through the wraith, who screams, but the sound is swallowed up as Max absorbs the spirit. The woman's body crumples to the floor.

Max changes back and I scoop him up, knowing he'll need the connection to me to recover. He clambers onto my shoulders and settles there.

Something moves in the shadows of the back door and we all whirl, but it's just an exhausted man leaning in the door frame, his hands bound and his wispy beard full of dust from lying on the floor.

"Oh, thank God," he says, adjusting his glasses best he can with his shoulder. "Now could you please untie me?"

After freeing who I surmise is Seamus the shopkeeper, Anna goes to retrieve her costume pieces. She returns with a black and silver mask and a strange look on her face, as if finding something somewhere other than where she'd left it.

"Well, that was certainly fun." Seamus brushes a layer of dust off his clothing. "Now, would someone please explain why there was a wraith in my shop?"

"Because you didn't ward it," Anna replies, holding the mask up to her face as if expecting to see something on the other side. Rose watches her with a curious tilt of her head.

Seamus looks unimpressed. "You brought a war inside."

"Technically the wraith brought it here," Anna replies, looping the mask around her uninjured wrist. Her injury appears to have stopped bleeding, the cloth wrapped tight, but I can see her wincing with each movement.

"Forget technicalities!" Seamus snaps, color beginning to build in his pale face. Max holds up a single paw, claws extended, and rakes it through the air, making a very distinct feisty meow sound.

I turn away to hide a smile, then grimace at the movement. With my fading adrenaline, the wound on my chest from the werewolf's claws has started to ache.

Anna sees it and winces, looking momentarily guilty. But what would she have to feel guilty about?

"My merchandise could have been damaged!" Seamus continues, and I take a giant step to the side to hide the sliced grim reaper costume.

Anna twirls the mask around her wrist. "I think the words you're looking for are 'thank you.' We could have just left."

Seamus tenses, the red that had appeared in his cheeks fading rapidly. He mutters something under his breath and stumbles ungracefully to a small counter in the corner that holds a single, age-old cash register.

Rose kneels beside the witch. "She'll wake soon. Will you tell her what happened?"

"Yeah, yeah," Seamus says with a wave.

Anna holds up the mask. "Do you know anything about this?"

He glances at the mask, then does a double take. "Well, that hasn't showed up for quite some time." He holds out his hand, opening and closing it impatiently. She sets the mask in his palm, and he turns it about, inspecting it with a chorus of tiny sounds of affirmation and curiosity.

"It's a Radharc," he says at last, setting it reverently down on the glass counter. When none of us react, he lets out an exasperated sigh and adds, "A mask that gives visions, though only one per wearer. Hasn't your father taught you anything?"

"What did you see?" I ask Anna.

She stiffens, and for a moment I get the strangest feeling she's about to lie to me. Then she says, "A man with dark hair and the greenest eyes I've ever seen. He was fighting a battle a long time ago." She shivers, as if the memory unnerves her.

"That sounds like the same man I saw," I say wonderingly. "But why did it give you a vision of Fin?"

Anna snatches up the mask, turning it over in her hand again as if it might suddenly reveal its inner workings.

"We should go," Rose says lightly. "There's still a third wraith out there somewhere."

We pay for our costume pieces—full price, since apparently saving Seamus from a wraith doesn't warrant a discount—and leave the shop. Rose doesn't remove her angel wings, somehow managing to slip into the driver's seat without the slightest problem.

"Are you okay?" Anna asks as I dab at the scratches on my chest with a towel Seamus gave me. Or rather, sold to me for a dollar. "What happened?"

I shake my head. "I don't know. I went to summon my Saint Knives, but I couldn't. The werewolf caught me while I was trying."

"Oh." Anna sinks a little lower in her seat.

Everyone's quiet after that. I squirm in the silence, feeling like there's a Jabberwocky in the room no one wants to talk about.

Eventually, I can't take it anymore.

"What the wraith said," I begin. "About me leading them to us—"

"She's lying," Anna cuts in before I can finish. "You're warded."

I want to believe her, but there's something in her voice. She sounds worried, and she keeps glancing at me in the rearview mirror. Max, who sits on my shoulder, gives my cheek a reassuring pat.

By the time we return to the house, it's nearing dinnertime and the rain has mostly subsided. The small parking lot down the driveway is fuller than when we left, and when we pull up into the roundabout, there's a young couple standing outside the front door. Their luggage is on the ground, their attention trained on something at their feet.

Rose parks beside the Charger on the side of the house. I exchange glances with Anna as we climb out of the car. Max leaps out after us, trailing us up the stairs.

"Do you need help getting checked in?" Anna asks. "I can—" She cuts off as we reach the couple's side.

Sitting in front of the door is a very damp, very dead raven.

Something between a snarl and a wail rises out of Max's throat, deep and guttural. His fur prickles up along his body. I feel both the urge to calm him and step away from him at the same time as the edges of his fur begin to flicker.

The rain starts again, abrupt and heavy. The couple beside us doesn't move, as if transfixed by the sight of the bird. Anna wraps an arm around her stomach, her fingers worrying at her lips.

Thunder erupts in the sky, shaking the couple out of their stupor.

"Just a practical joke." The man laughs, sliding his arm over his wife's shoulders. "It's probably rubber." He reaches out to nudge it with his toe, and Max roars, his body rippling.

The man recoils. His wife's face goes white as the lightning.

Over the patter of the rain and the snarl of the thunder, I can hear the man and his wife talking hurriedly to themselves. They gather their luggage, racing off the porch back the way they came.

Rose carefully picks up Max, cradling him to her chest. She

rocks him softly with the wind while he howls as if in pain, the rain pouring harder than it has in days.

"It's a Jabberwocky," Anna says quietly. Her brows are drawn to a point as she chews her lower lip.

"They're nearly impossible to kill." She points at the raven. "Whatever did this is really powerful. It's . . . it's got to be him. Kaden's boss. He's back."

CHAPTER 18

Anna

The front door flies open and Aunt Elaine barrels onto the porch. "I sensed—" She stops when she sees the dead raven and Rose cradling Max. Then her gaze lands on my wounded arm. "Get inside. Now."

We obey, the door swinging shut behind us. Aunt Elaine ushers us into the library, where Nora paces before the fire. Relief fills her face when she sees me, and she wraps me in a hug.

"You're okay," she breathes. "I had a terrible vision of the costume shop. The costumes—"

"Came to life." I hold up my injured arm. "Yeah, I know."

Nora's eyes widen and she guides me onto the couch. Rose hands Max to Colin and joins us, her medical supplies in hand. She unwraps my arm, revealing a shallow wound that's mostly stopped bleeding, though it stings a lot.

"What happened?" Nora demands when Colin joins us by the fire.

He recounts the attack while Rose cleans and bandages my arm, his voice faltering when he mentions what the wraith said about him being the reason they were discovered.

"She wouldn't tell us how," I say as Rose ties off the bandage, then shifts over to work on the scratches on Colin's collarbone.

"I'm sorry," Colin says quietly. "Anna got hurt because of me."

His words are a gut punch. I'm pretty sure that *he* got hurt because of *me*. What if the journal locking down when I tried to draw in it is what stopped him from being able to summon his Saint Knives?

Aunt Elaine folds her arms. "No, you should have been untraceable with your warding."

The library door opens, and Uncle Roy enters. He's nearly soaked through, but a moment later the water goes up in steam as he uses his pyrokinesis. "Perimeter's clear," he says, pushing his hair out of his face. "No guests saw anything, and I've . . . seen to the raven."

Max curls tighter in Colin's arms, burying his face into the crook of his elbow. Rose sticks a big Band-Aid over Colin's collarbone and starts cleaning up her supplies. There are tears in her eyes, and I know she can feel Max's pain as if it's her own.

Uncle Roy hovers awkwardly in the doorway. He clearly has something else to say, and Nora gives him an expectant look. "It's nothing. Only, well, you know how hard Jabberwockies are to kill. With their strength, a member of the Ravenguard could wear one down enough to do it, not that they would, and other than that . . ." He shrugs one massive shoulder. "Anything left on the list isn't something I want to face."

Kara gives me a look that clearly says, *You haven't told them yet?*

And I glance at Colin. We're withholding important information from the adults that could tie all of this together. He gives me a nod.

"Colin had a vision of a man named Fin Varra when he fainted from the wraith poison," I say. "And at the costume shop, I found a Radharc that showed me a vision of him."

Nora looks alarmed. "Why didn't you tell me this?"

I wince. "I didn't want to worry you."

"Anna—" She pinches the bridge of her nose. "Don't you see? Fin Varra is the Irish King of the Dead. Dead, as in *wraiths*. He must be the one behind all of this. He's helping the wraiths absorb people's souls. He's hunting down Ravens."

"But that doesn't explain why Colin had a vision of him," I start, and just as quickly stop when I realize what about my vision in the costume shop bothered me so much: the knives Fin had been holding—they were *Saint Knives*!

And one of them had a tiny, cat-ear-shaped nick in the handle, just like Colin's.

Raven journals are passed down through generations. What if those Saint Knives had been in there for centuries? What if they'd once *belonged* to Fin?

"Oh no," I whisper. All eyes turn to me, and I hesitate, not wanting to make things worse.

Kara, on the other hand, has no reservations. She plucks the words right out of my head. "Fin was holding a pair of Saint Knives in Anna's vision that had the same chip in the handle as Colin's. She thinks Colin's family is descended from Fin Varra, which would explain why Colin got a vision of Fin when he used the knives, and why Anna saw Fin when she looked at Colin through the Radharc— Hey!"

The pillow I chucked at her rebounds uselessly off her shoulder, and it's all I can do not to find something more solid to throw.

Kara's words leave the adults' faces stunned and Colin looking nauseous.

"Perhaps that is why you feel so ancient to me." Rose lifts a hand, feeling the air about Colin. "His magic runs through you."

Unease unfurls in my belly when Nora and Aunt Elaine exchange another worried glance. "We don't even know if this is true!"

"I'm afraid it is." Gran enters the library, a burning candle in her hand. The tip of the flame is pointing directly at Colin. "On a hunch, I performed a séance to locate Mr. Varra, but his presence is in the Otherworld. Instead, my spell has led me here, to Mr. Pierce."

We all look as one to Colin, who shrinks beneath our gazes. "What does that mean?"

"It means you share the same energy, which is why my séance spell brought me to you," Gran replies. "Anna's theory is correct: you are Mr. Varra's descendant."

Colin's eyes widen, and he wilts into the couch. I can only imagine what he's thinking: he's not only descended from an ancient Irish deity, but his own ancestor is responsible for the deaths of countless Ravens, including his parents.

"But if Fin's in the Otherworld, how could he have killed Colin's parents?" I ask. "We both saw him in the motel room. He was definitely here."

Gran sets her candle down on the nearest windowsill, and the house snuffs out the flame, rattling the window frame in an unusual display of annoyance at Gran. "I suspect that similar to a Jabberwocky, Mr. Varra isn't able to stay in the human world long.

When Mr. Pierce's older brother wounded him so severely, he was forced to return to the Otherworld to recover while his wraiths remained here to bolster their ranks."

"There's more," Rose says softly.

Nora looks from her to her mom. "What aren't you saying?"

Gran's face grows grim. "I'm sure Mr. Pierce would never intentionally harm us, but I fear his connection to Mr. Varra is what enabled his wraiths to track him and Anna to the costume shop where they were attacked, resulting in both their injuries."

Nora shoots Aunt Elaine a sharp *I told you so* look, and Uncle Roy stares at Gran openmouthed.

Colin pales, but Gran doesn't stop there. "There's no telling how strong their connection is," she says. "I fear . . . well, I fear Mr. Varra may be able to act *through* him."

My first instinct is to tell her she's out of her mind, but then I think about my nightmare, and about the Radharc, and how it only showed me Fin when I looked at Colin. And Gran—I've never seen her this way. Her face is so serious. She wouldn't say this unless she was sure. No one knows more about magic than Gran.

"Is that really possible, Ma?" Uncle Roy asks, breaking the mounting silence. "I mean, wouldn't Fin have possessed him already?"

"I believe he might have." Gran's gaze drops to Max, who at some point crept closer to the fire to curl up, and I realize with a sinking sensation what she means.

Members of the Ravenguard are strong enough to kill Jabberwockies.

Colin must realize it, too, because he's shaking his head. "I didn't. I wouldn't!"

"You wouldn't have had a choice, lad," Gran says.

"He's been with us all day!" I say.

Gran gives me a pitying look. "That Jabberwocky has been dead for more than a day. The possession probably occurred at night when you were all asleep, and then a wraith delivered the corpse to our doorstep."

Colin leaps to his feet. I grab his hand, wanting to reassure him, but the spot goes icy cold. I have one terrible second to recognize the feeling of an oncoming vision before it envelops me.

I'm stalking through the woods, my footfalls soft in the underbrush. The blackened trees bend in welcome; the wind sings my name.

The Jabberwocky slumbers beneath the silver oak, no longer in raven form. I am as quiet as the leaves, as silent as the night.

I plunge my knives into its throat.

I rip free of the vision, nearly tumbling off the couch. Nora catches me, her hands cold against my hot skin. For a moment I think the sky is thundering outside, but then I realize the sound is my heart pounding. My vision clears, revealing Colin crouching in front of me, his gray eyes wide.

"Colin," I whisper, and he must understand from my voice, because he looks ill.

He shakes his head. "But I don't remember. I . . . I couldn't have."

"You wouldn't remember anything you did under his command," Gran says grimly. From the look on everyone's faces, they must realize what I saw too.

Gran sighs heavily. "I'm sorry, Mr. Pierce. But I think until we sort this out, it's best if you leave Ravenfall."

"Ma," Aunt Elaine says in shock.

"We need Colin, though," Uncle Roy appeals. "He's a good

kid, a good fighter, and our only link to Fin. Samhain is the most likely time for Fin to make his move, and if he shows up at the masquerade when everyone's wearing a mask, how will we find him?"

"Plus his glamour!" I add. "It was so strong in the vision, so we have no idea what he looks like."

"We'll have you to find him, Anna," Gran says, and for half a second something about the way she says it feels strange.

"What? Me?" I ask. "What can I do? My powers are useless."

"Psychometry is one of the rarest and most powerful abilities known to psychics," Gran says. "Mr. Varra's glamour may work against Rose's empathy and Kara's telepathy, but not you. To find him, all you have to do is touch him, and you'll get a vision of Mr. Pierce's parents' deaths. Then we'll know who Mr. Varra is, and the rest of us can subdue him and force him to cross back to the Otherworld. Keeping Mr. Pierce here is too big of a risk."

Something about what she's saying pulls at me. I don't want to believe Colin is a danger to us, but I can't ignore the evidence. Maybe we don't need him. I should be protecting the inn anyway. It's my home, my responsibility.

Maybe, for once, we just need me.

Guilt creeps through me at the thoughts, but I can't shut them out. I've been waiting for an opportunity to prove that my powers are useful for so long. Colin staying here might ruin all of that, and yet telling him to leave feels wrong.

"They're right." Colin's voice cracks. I can tell he's trying to be strong. I want to tell him he doesn't have to, but the words won't come.

He shakes his head. "I couldn't even defend myself, Anna, let alone you. The one time I needed my powers, I couldn't even summon something. I'm a danger to you all. I should go."

"But—" I start, the truth on the tip of my tongue, but stop when Nora lays a hand on my shoulder.

"Let him go, honey," she says gently. "It's just until we figure things out."

Uncle Roy steps up beside him. "Come on, I know just the place."

CHAPTER 19

Colin

Everything happens so quickly.

I gather my things from my room, packing them all into my battered old bag. It isn't until I zip it closed that I realize part of me had hoped I'd never need to pack it again.

Part of me had hoped I'd found a home, that maybe when Liam returned, we could stay here forever.

I hold my breath, refusing to let my emotions get the better of me as I rejoin Roy on the front porch in the biting evening air. He offers me an apologetic look, and I want to tell him it's okay, that I'm fine, but the words won't come out. We climb into his truck in silence.

The last image I see as we circle around the drive is the Charger sitting in the dark.

My thoughts hound me the whole way, as merciless as the rain pounding against the truck's windows. The windshield wipers screech with each brush across the glass, punctuating each thought:

I'm descended from the King of the Dead.

Screech.

Because of me, Anna got hurt.

Screech.

I might have killed Max's friend.

Screech.

I stare down at my hands and imagine them coated in blood.

Roy fiddles with the radio, but only static comes through, and he eventually turns it off. The whine of the windshield wipers and the hum of the truck's snow tires on the wet highway fill the silence.

It only takes a few minutes to reach town. Roy turns the truck down a series of side streets before pulling into the parking lot with a glowing neon sign that reads, WHEN IN WICK and below it, MOTEL.

Something cold and broken in me actually laughs, and Roy gives me an uneasy look. I realize he might think Fin is doing something to me now, but I don't have the energy left to explain that my life apparently begins and ends with motels.

He pulls the truck into a parking space and cuts the engine.

"A, uh, friend of ours owns this place," he says after a moment's silence. "A witch. It's warded, so you should be safe."

I stare at the bag wedged between my knees and wonder if I'll ever stop running.

Roy unbuckles his seat belt, angling toward me in his seat. "Listen, lad, I know this is tough. None of it's your fault, though, you hear me? It's just . . . well, rotten luck."

"Yeah," I say. "I get a lot of that."

Before he can respond, I wrench open the truck door and leap out, towing my bag after me.

"Hold on," Roy says. "I'll come in with you."

"Don't," I reply. "I know what I'm doing."

Slamming the door, I trudge up to the visitor's entrance, where the only light flickers and groans.

A dark-skinned woman with tight black curls and a round, kindly face is sitting behind the counter when I enter. She wears a Star of David necklace and is shifting through an assortment of crystals. The room smells lightly of incense and is neat and clean with dark upholstery and stained glass, like an old Irish pub.

"Are you Colin?" she asks in a richly timbered voice, already reaching for a room key. "Room's paid through," she adds when I dig into my pocket in hopes of finding cash.

"No magic or supernatural visitors in the rooms." She taps a crystal with a wink. "I'll know. Room's down the hall to the left. Name's Alice if you need anything."

I take the key from her. "Thanks."

I step back into the chill night air to find Roy waiting for me with an overnight bag. He catches my confused expression. "You didn't think we were going to leave you here alone, did you?"

"Why not? Everyone else did." The words are out before I can stop them. But it's true. I'm sick of being left behind.

Roy doesn't seem to know what to say, so I follow the corridor to the room. Inside are two queen beds bracketed by nightstands, a low dresser with a TV, and a bathroom. I toss my bag on a bed and pick up a takeout menu someone left on the nightstand.

Half an hour later and we each have a steaming carton with a hamburger and fries. Roy devours his, but as I sit on the bed, the heat of the food seeping out of the carton and into my hands, my appetite is gone.

All I want is to be sitting in the ballroom at Ravenfall, drinking Wish Cider and laughing with Anna. But I know I made the right decision. Staying there put her and her family in danger, and if I've learned anything the last few weeks, it's that people die around me. First my parents, maybe Liam, too, and now Max's friend.

Being around me is dangerous—especially when I can't even use my powers.

I say as much to Roy, hoping he'll return to Ravenfall where it's safe, but expecting him to just laugh me off. He does neither.

Instead, he sets his food aside and joins me on my bed. "Has anyone told you the story of why your parents left the trade?"

I shake my head, and he takes a deep breath, settling his hands in his lap where they spark nervously. "It was my fault."

That gets my attention. I angle toward him to listen.

"I'm the youngest of our lot. Elaine's nearly eight years older than me, same as your parents, and Nora about six," he says. "Despite that, the five of us were pretty good friends, though I always felt a little like I was tagging along from behind."

Now that's a feeling I get. The last week has had me feeling left behind in the dust, as if all the world were in on a secret only I didn't know, because no one thought I could handle it.

"I told you before that Elaine and I sometimes trained with your parents and some local Ravens who taught them, but what I didn't say is how much I longed to be a real Raven. Your parents indulged me, especially Bridget." Here, he smiles softly before continuing. "But they never actually let me go out on hunts with them."

"Too dangerous," I mutter, the same reason they never told me the truth.

He nods. "They were right, but I didn't see that at the time. I was barely fifteen and desperate to prove I could do everything they could. So one night I went out into the woods with a bundle of bluebells intending to call some faeries. Just something harmless that I could capture and bring home."

My stomach begins to sink as I see where his story is going.

"I got a redcap instead." He shivers at the memory. "Nasty creatures. The only thing they care about is finding the next source of blood to wet their cap. I was in over my head and running for my life when Bridget found me. Nora'd had a vision of me in danger."

I'm fully facing him now, enraptured by his story.

"Turns out the blood of a Raven is a mighty powerful thing to a redcap." Roy's hands wring in his lap, the sparks coming quicker. "One, Bridget could handle, but the redcap had friends. She fought three of them on her own until your father and Elaine got there. By the time the redcaps were dead, your mother could barely stand. We almost didn't get her to the hospital in time."

He swallows hard, looking at me for the first time. "I didn't find out until later that she was pregnant with your brother, Liam. She almost lost him. When they found out what I'd done, Niall exploded."

That sounds just like Dad. He was the easiest-going person I knew—until it came to his family.

"Nora and Elaine defended me, and things escalated from there," Roy says. "By the end of the week they'd sold their house in Wick and packed up the truck. We haven't heard from them since."

That's why my parents never went to the Ballinkays for help. That's why Roy had looked so guilty when Nora said maybe they didn't think they could.

"I'm going to do what I can to make up for that mistake," Roy says, standing. "Now you're the one in danger, and I'm going to keep you safe. I owe your parents a lot more than that."

I want those words to warm me up, to comfort me, but all I can think about are the differences in our stories. When everything went wrong for him, it wasn't his fault, not really.

This is all on me.

Leaving was the right choice, I think. But as I stare at my rapidly cooling dinner in its white takeout container, my bag tucked beneath my feet, all I can think is the same thing in a hundred different words: *forsaken, forlorn, deserted.*

Alone.

CHAPTER 20

Anna

I wake the next morning feeling like something is missing.

It's only when I roll to the side to find Max sleeping beside me that I remember: Colin's gone.

For a moment I just lie there, looking at the glowing plastic stars on my ceiling and wrestling with a squirming feeling in my belly. Last night is an uncomfortable wedge between my ribs, but I didn't know what else to do. Gran is never wrong about this kind of stuff.

I try to tell myself that it's what's best, that I can do this myself, but the more I repeat it, the faker it sounds.

Sighing, I slide out of bed and try to coax Max to follow, but he won't lift his head, even when I tell him breakfast is ready. That really worries me. The only person who loves food more than Colin around here is Max.

I wince at the thought of Colin. I hope he's okay.

The day drags on as Nora assigns me chore after chore in preparation for tomorrow's party. The inn is nearly full to bursting with guests, and I weave between them as I dust and turn down rooms with the house's help. With so many people around, it's impossible to avoid everyone, and by the end of the afternoon, I've seen a couple things I rather I hadn't.

I try to focus on how nice the house is starting to look, wrapped in faerie lights and tall orange lanterns, the windowsills lined with bouquets of autumn flowers and tiny pumpkins that Colin and I drew faces on days ago, but it all feels hollow.

I trudge into dinner in the ballroom that evening feeling low. As much as I want to, I can't shake the heavy feeling that's welled up inside me. As if sensing my mood, the dining room is subdued. The tiny lights dangling above like suspended raindrops are a dull yellow, and the mist the house usually draws inside and weaves into shapes floats lifelessly near the vaulted ceiling.

If I didn't know any better, I'd say it's as down as I am.

If the guests can sense the house's somber mood, they don't show it. We're near to capacity, the big round tables throughout filled with people laughing and talking.

I get food from the buffet and join my family at our table but only draw shapes in my mashed potatoes. As I scan the faces seated around the table, I realize it's not just Colin's absence that has my stomach in knots: it's dread of what's to come. What we're dealing with is dangerous, and we're down a set of helping hands.

Aunt Elaine and Uncle Roy can defend themselves, but so could Colin's parents, and they're dead. What about Nora? Rose? Kara? My stomach clenches as I think of each one, unable to stop myself from imagining them like Colin's parents: with their eyes empty.

The rain hasn't slowed at all. It pounds against the floor-to-ceiling windows without mercy. The thunder shakes even the trees outside, and I'm sure the only reason the house isn't vibrating is because it's trying really hard not to.

A particularly bright strike of lightning illuminates the ballroom, and Aunt Elaine lets out a low whistle. "He's going to bring the inn down at this rate."

"Poor Max." Rose bows her head.

"I always thought the connection between Jabberwockies' emotions and the weather was an old wives' tale," Kara adds, staring out the window at the trees bending in the wind.

I follow her gaze, and in the faint glow of the house's lights, I see a small black form, nearly invisible in the gathering dark.

Pushing back my chair, I ignore Nora's call and head out the rear door. Across the field by the wood, Max sits before two gnarled oak trees that have grown around each other, their bodies twisted together. There's a small mound of fresh dirt by his paws, and he sits hunched over with his shoulders rigid and his tail curled tightly around his body.

The rain pelts me with freezing droplets as I kneel beside him, gently placing a hand on his back. He leans into me, and I nearly flinch at how cold and wet he is. He must have been out here for hours.

"It'll be okay, Max," I say softly, even though nothing feels as if it's going to be okay.

Max lifts his head, one green eye slanting at me, and in it I see the depthless, ancient creature he really is, torn and bereft at the loss of a friend.

Gran said we didn't need Colin, that we could do this ourselves. That I could do this myself. But sitting there in the pouring rain with Max, the wind howling around us, I realize I don't want to do it alone.

I want my friend here.

The knot in my chest loosens a little at the realization. Max nudges my hand with his head, and I gather him into my arms, squeezing gently.

Then someone curses behind us.

I turn, searching the dark. The sound was almost lost in the wind, but I spot a hunched figure at the kitchen entrance, fighting with the door handle. The house shudders, the door snapping shut beneath the woman's hands. She shouts something at it, then rips the door open and stumbles inside.

Max and I exchange a glance; then we're off after her. I get to the porch just in time to glimpse Gran exiting the kitchen. Why would the house be trying to keep Gran out? The only person it likes more than me is her.

We sneak through the kitchen after her, following her up the steps to the fourth-floor bedroom she uses when she visits. She fumbles with the door again.

"Gran?" I call.

She turns, and a shiver that has nothing to do with the cold creeps down my spine.

"Anna, how nice to see you." Her airy voice flutters past us. "I'm afraid I can't talk right now."

This time I realize why my name sounds wrong.

She *never* just calls me Anna.

A low growl reverberates in Max's throat, and Gran freezes. Slowly, a too-wide smile spreads across her face. "Now, now, we're not going to hurt dear ole grandma, are we?"

Her eyes flash silver and I gasp—the third wraith from Kara's surveillance photo. "How long have you been possessing her?"

The wraith laughs. "She's a recent acquisition. Needed a little convincing." It pushes up Gran's sleeve, revealing deep claw-shaped gouges on her forearm like those Kaden gave Colin. Ink-black lines run up the veins of her arm.

The wraith poisoned her—that was how it'd been able to possess her despite her wards.

My mind races, trying to make sense of everything. "Then all that stuff you said about Colin. None of it was true."

"But you just ate it up, didn't you, *Anna-love*?" The forced grin is still plastered across her face. "Jealousy is never a good look."

My hands curl into fists. "Get out of her!"

"Oh, I'm quite comfortable. I think I'll stay awhile—see what her magic can do. And without your Raven here to save you . . ."

"Max," I say, scooting back to give him room.

His body morphs in a single smooth movement, and a low, keening cry erupts from his throat. Gran screams and slams her hands over her ears. Max cries again and the wraith begins to twitch and jerk. Black and white light appears around her skin, gathering shape. Max calls a third time, and the shape of the spirit's body erupts from Gran's, looking as if it's trying to tear itself away.

Max turns translucent and steps through Gran. The wraith's spirit rips from her, a scream echoing down the hall, before it disappears entirely.

Gran gasps, stumbling to the side, but Max is there, his body solid once again. He curls around her to hold her upright.

"Oh." She places a hand against him, steadying herself. "Thank you, Maxwell."

I rush to her side. "Gran! Are you okay?" She takes my hand, allowing me to help her toward her room.

"I'd say so," Gran replies breathlessly. "It was certainly an experience."

Max transforms back and trots after us, licking his maw in satisfaction. A door opens and a guest pokes out his head. "I know this place is going for authentic and all, but can you tone down the screaming? It doesn't even sound real."

Max snarls at him—the sound of a Jabberwocky, not a cat—and the man pales, retreating quickly into his room. I hear the dead bolt slide home.

I get Gran settled in a chair by the window of her room, and the house starts a small fire in the hearth. It makes me nervous to have any sort of heat in the room, as the whole thing is piled high with books. Books on shelves, books in stacks on the floor, books in dirt-less flowerpots and stuffed into nooks and crannies along the walls and inside the décor.

The pure disorganization of it all nearly gives me a headache, but I know Colin would love it.

"Bibliophile," I mutter to myself.

As if sensing what's on my mind, Gran lays a gentle hand on my arm. "It's not your fault, dear. You didn't know."

I shake my head, suddenly feeling as if I might cry. "I was so ready to believe it. I felt like he was stealing my attention."

I never should have let them send Colin away. He only agreed to go because he thought he was useless, that he'd failed as a Raven, but it's because of *me* that he couldn't use his powers. *I'm* the one who broke his connection to the journal.

"I messed up, Gran," I say.

She squeezes my arm. "Everyone does, Anna-love. What matters is what you do next."

"We have to tell everyone what happened," I say, determined to make this right. "They have to know the wraith was lying. Colin's not really a danger to us, is he?"

"No, he isn't." Gran sighs, settling in her chair. "There was some truth in what that creature said: Colin is descended from Fin, and they possess a bond. It's how his wraiths were able to find him despite his warding, but he cannot use that connection to act through Colin."

"But my vision of the Jabberwocky?"

A sorrowful look fills her expression. "It was a false memory that the wraith planted in Colin's mind, through me. Kaden killed the Jabberwocky, not him."

Colin had looked so devastated when he thought he'd killed Max's friend, but he hadn't had anything to do with it. None of this was his fault, and we'd sent him away.

"There's more." With a wave of her hand, Gran summons a book from atop a nearby stack. It hovers before her, flipping to a page toward the middle, before spinning midair to face me, revealing the thorn-covered Triskelion.

"Most spirits who reach the Otherworld do so through death. But Fin and his people crossed over not as spirits, but *alive* in their mortal bodies. Bodies that have long since withered and died, leaving their spirits trapped for thousands of years. The Otherworld is not a kind place. Fin's people may have been like you and me when they walked in, but if they come out, there will be nothing left of who they once were. The impact their spiritual presence will have on the balance of the three realms will be disastrous."

"The three realms?" I ask.

The book's pages flip of their own accord. "Creation, preservation, destruction," Gran reads. Then beneath it in Irish, "The celestial world, the human world, and the Otherworld. The meanings among the Triskelion are intertwined, as are the three worlds. There is a delicate balance among them that if broken would mean disaster for all three."

The book closes and settles on a nearby stack. "I remember bits and pieces of my time possessed by that wraith, and from what I've learned, I suspect that Fin's true plan is to destroy the Shield and free his people's spirits."

That's why they've been killing Ravens: to weaken the Shield enough that Fin will be able to destroy it on Samhain, when he and his wraiths are at their most powerful and the Shield is at its weakest. But if the Shield falls, it won't just be Fin's people who are freed: it'll be every spirit and dangerous supernatural creature in the Otherworld.

"Maybe he won't be recovered in time," I suggest hopefully. "Liam wounded him badly enough that he had to return to the Otherworld to recover. Maybe he'll be too weak to complete his plan."

Gran's expression hardens. "I wish that were the case, but I suspect Kaden hasn't just been gathering wraiths to bolster the ranks. As King of the Dead, Fin can absorb the life forces of others to sustain himself, as he did when he killed Colin's parents. I believe the other wraiths are possessing their host bodies so that when Fin crosses over to our world, he'll be able to absorb their life forces enough to finish healing."

A sense of growing dread creeps up my neck. "Which will make them permanent residents, same as Kaden." But why did Fin care about giving these spirits new bodies? Unless . . . "You said Fin wants to free his people's spirits, and that a wraith's motivations are tied to who they were in life. Then Kaden and the others—they aren't random spirits! They're the spirits of Fin's people. When he breaks the Shield, they'll possess new hosts, and Fin will absorb their hosts' life forces, giving them new bodies."

Gran nods, looking troubled. "The question is whether they've removed enough Ravens to weaken the Shield enough to destroy it."

Cold realization descends on me. "This was all a trick to get Colin out of the house. They're going to kill him!"

CHAPTER 21

Colin

R ain pelts our motel room window hard enough to make it rattle. My cup of lobby tea went cold on my nightstand hours ago, and the heat is busted, but I don't mind the cold. It keeps me awake.

Roy alternates between walking the perimeter and doing work on his laptop, and I spend the day flipping through static-filled TV channels and making my way through my forgotten dictionary. For a moment, it almost felt like old times. As though my parents were going to walk through that door exhausted but smiling with takeout from whatever local place was still open past nine.

But as the evening set in and the storm worsened, no one came.

Some part of me knows that I need to come up with a plan. I can't just lie here forever hoping Liam will show and waiting for news from Ravenfall. Even if they defeat Fin tomorrow night, and it's safe for me to leave, my reasons for staying there will be gone. I'll have to move on.

It hurts to think.

Ravenfall had started to feel like home, and I'd forgotten that I couldn't just stay there forever and expect them to take care of me.

Still, I hate that I can't be there to help them. I hate that there's so much happening outside of my control, that I'm a danger to people I care about, and that even if it was only for a moment, they'd looked afraid of me.

All at once, everything bubbles up inside me. My grief over losing my parents and Liam's disappearance, my fear at being thrust into the world alone and confused, my anger at the secrets that have been kept from me, and most of all, the pain of leaving Ravenfall.

With Roy outside our room on a perimeter check and no one else there to tell me I'm being immature, or to look at me with pity I can't take, I finally cry. My body shakes and my breath catches, and I press my palms to my eyes, but I can't stop.

For so long, I've needed to be strong. First for my parents, so as not to burden them with even more. Then for myself, to get answers about my past and find Liam. But as my nose grows stuffy and my throat begins to ache, I wonder if holding everything in ever really made me strong, or if it just made me hurt all the more.

By the time I stop crying, I feel emptied out, like a pumpkin scooped of its guts. In the place of all those emotions is a single one: determination.

Firmness of purpose, I think as I roll out of bed and fish the journal out of my bag.

Even when my parents were here, I'd never been good at sitting around doing nothing. Now, with people I care about in danger because of me, there has to be *something* I can do.

Fin's people found me because of the link between us. If I leave the motel, I can draw him out and defeat him a whole day before Samhain. Then the Ballinkays won't be in danger.

But first, I need to figure out what's wrong with my magic.

The journal feels strange in my hands, dead and cold. When I try to pry it open, it doesn't budge, as if someone glued all the pages together. This must be why I couldn't summon the Saint Knives at the shop: the journal has locked me out.

"Okay," I say aloud, forcing myself to stay calm. "If it's locked, then I need a key."

I think back to the words Elaine had me say when I first bonded with the journal, and repeat them the best I can now, the Irish awkward on my tongue.

Nothing happens.

"Come on!" I knock the journal against the bed, the motion making my chest twinge with pain. My hand goes to the wound on reflex and comes away with blood; it's leaking through the bandage.

"Great." I start to slide off the bed to head for the bathroom but stop, an idea occurring to me. This journal is bonded to my family, and there's only one thing everyone in my family shares. Hoping I'm not about to stain a thousand-year-old antique passed down through generations of my family, I press my bloody finger to the trinity knot embossed on the cover.

At first, nothing.

Then the blood seeps into the page, and something shifts like a mechanism. The connection between me and the journal springs back into place in a welcoming rush. My shoulders slump with relief and I flip through the pages, looking for clues about why it shut me out, but it looks the same as ever.

I focus on the feel of my Saint Knives in my free hand. They materialize, the metal cool to the touch. In one, the handle has a triangular chip, like a vampire's fang. I run my finger over it. Did Fin wield these in battle? Did they sustain that mark defending him and his people?

It's hard to imagine the warrior in my vision thoughtlessly killing people. There'd been something so regal about him, something that demanded respect. What had changed?

Drawing a fortifying breath, I shove the thoughts aside and stand. Whatever led Fin to become the monster he is now doesn't matter—stopping him does.

I wrench open the door. The rain has quieted, a heavy fog seeping through the motel parking lot, patches illuminated bright orange and red by the flashing neon signs. My Saint Knives are comfortable in my hands as I step out, leaving behind the protection wards. The motel is quiet, the lights of the other rooms dim. There's no sign of Roy.

If I wait long enough, Fin or his wraiths will find me.

Cold night air seeps through my jacket, and I take deep breaths to keep myself calm. I don't know what to expect. The man in my vision had been strong, a warrior. Can I really stand up to someone that powerful?

The wind howls, rattling the VACANCY sign hanging overhead. Another sound scratches below it. I tighten my grip, listening harder, but the scream of the wind and scrape of the sign are too loud.

I feel the press of eyes at my back and turn but find only swirling mist.

A distant humming fills the air. I try to find the source, but the fog is so thick, and the light plays off it in strange ways. Then something moves in the darkness.

I have my knives raised before the shape solidifies into Alice, the motel clerk. She holds a pulsing purple crystal in one hand, her face serious.

"You shouldn't be out here," she says.

"I'm—" I start, then stop. What could I possibly say? I'm waiting for the King of the Dead so I can defeat him before my friends are put in mortal danger?

It's not that I don't think she'll believe me—she's a witch, after all—but she'll probably tow me right back inside.

The purple crystal glows brighter, and her brow furrows. "Something has its eye on you."

A shiver runs down my spine. Then a high-pitched screech cuts the air, followed by a flood of light and the sound of creaking metal.

I lift my blades, ready to fight, blood pounding in my ears.

Then a familiar voice says, "Colin? Colin, what is it?"

I blink against the brightness, which I realize now is a set of headlights from a car that had come screeching into the parking lot.

Then my gaze settles on Anna hanging out the passenger window, her dark eyes wide with alarm. Elaine leans around her from the driver's seat to ask, "Are they here?"

Lowering my knives, I shake my head, and Anna leaps out of the car. "Get your stuff," she says. "We need to get back to Ravenfall."

"But Fin—"

"I'll explain on the way. Hurry!"

I look to Alice, who stows her crystal in her pocket with a nod. Banishing my knives to the journal, I dive into my room, where my bag waits neatly packed, always ready to go. Roy barrels in a moment later, clearly having gotten the rundown from Anna.

"What were you thinking?" he demands, shoving his stuff into his overnight bag.

"I wasn't!"

"Clearly!" He stops, his full attention on me. "Promise me you won't ever do something like that again, Colin."

I bite my lip but nod, and Roy looks at me a moment longer, as if he doesn't really believe me. I don't know if I do either.

Once Roy has the last of his things, we duck outside, where Alice has cast a shimmering protection spell over the parking lot. I join Elaine and Anna in the car, and Roy gets into his truck.

"Thanks, Alice," Roy says through the open window. "See you at the party?"

Her eyes flick into the dark. "Go quickly."

Elaine doesn't need telling twice. "Buckle up," she says, and hits the gas.

I obey just as she tears out onto the street, Roy's truck on our tail. Anna twists around in her seat to look at me. "What were you doing out there?" she demands.

"Trying to draw out Fin," I reply. Saying it out loud makes me feel suddenly stupid.

Anna's face tells me she agrees. "And why in the world would you want to do that?"

"I thought—" I stop, shame rising hot in my cheeks. I'd thought if I defeated him, I'd be a hero. That there'd be no reason for me to stay in that motel any longer and I could go back to Ravenfall.

That maybe I could stay.

Anna's expression softens, and I wonder if she knows what I'm thinking without asking. She might not be telepathic, but she's gotten to know me more over the last couple weeks than anyone has in a long time besides my family.

"It wasn't you, Colin," she says gently. "You didn't kill the Jabberwocky."

"What?" I listen in shock as she explains about Gran and the wraith that possessed her, how Fin never left the Otherworld after Liam wounded him.

"Kaden killed the Jabberwocky," Anna finishes solemnly. "Fin never took control of you. It was all a trick to get you out of the house so his wraiths could get to you. The more Ravens they kill, the weaker the Shield will be on Samhain, and the easier it'll be for Fin to destroy it."

Elaine gives me an apologetic smile in the rearview mirror. "We're so sorry, Colin. We're so used to taking everything my mother says as scripture that we got ahead of ourselves. We're glad to have you back."

It wasn't me. I wasn't the problem.

I slump in my seat, suddenly boneless, and my next breath feels like the first in years. As the warmth and woodsmoke scent of the car hit me, so does the relief. It sweeps through me, carrying away the adrenaline and fear that drove me into that parking lot.

"What about my powers?" I ask. "At the costume shop—"

"That was my fault." Anna bows her head. "I wanted to draw something in your journal for you, but it locked me out. I panicked and thought if I gave it back to you, it'd be fine, but I guess it messed with your connection. I'm sorry."

"Anna," Elaine chastises, and she winces.

That was why I hadn't been able to open the journal. I hadn't failed at using my powers at all, but I'd been so quick to doubt myself, I didn't stop to think of other possibilities.

I let out a heavy sigh of relief. "It's okay," I say, because it is. "It's fixed now, and you were only trying to help."

She turns and smiles at me in the rearview mirror. "So were you."

She means leaving and trying to face Fin on my own. Both of us wanted to do something useful, to help, but we'd tried to do it alone when we should have leaned on each other.

I focus on that thought as we trace our way back to Ravenfall and up the long, forest-lined drive to the mismatched house.

Max is waiting for us on the porch.

My feet barely strike the ground before he bounds over and leaps at me. I catch him against my chest, his little body soft and warm and crackling with a low purr.

"I missed you too," I tell him, and for the first time in my life, arriving at an inn doesn't feel like starting over again.

It feels like coming home.

We head for the library, where we find the twins, Nora, and Gran sitting by the fire. Nora and Gran both stand with matching apologetic looks on their faces.

"We're so sorry, Colin," Nora says. "I was scared, and too quick to react."

"And I let my guard down," Gran says with a bow of her head. "That wraith shouldn't have gotten near me."

Their apologies are the warmth of a fire after a cold rain, and the last of the tension in my chest fades. "It's okay," I say, and look to Nora. "You were only doing what you thought was best."

Nora lays a gentle hand on my shoulder. "I told you that you were welcome here for as long as you wanted, and I meant it. We should never have sent you away." She enfolds me in a hug, and it's so strong, so comforting, that I never want her to let go.

"All right, Nor, don't smother the poor kid!" Roy claps me on the shoulder as Nora releases me with a warm smile.

"We need a plan for Samhain." Elaine stands before the fire, her arms crossed as we all join the twins on the couches. "We know who we're up against now, and we know what he wants: to destroy the Shield. With Ravenfall being a weak spot in the Shield, this is the best place for them to strike, and we know they're coming for Colin. It's safe to assume they'll be at the party tomorrow night."

Nora's fingers worry at her mouth as she says, "Our first step is to identify him."

"I know it was the wraith talking, but Gran's plan with Anna's powers still makes sense to me," Colin says. "She just has to touch Fin at the party, and she'll get the same vision she did when she touched me."

Kara snorts loudly. "Have you ever been to— Oh, no, I guess you haven't. Well, there are *a lot* of people here on Samhain."

"Anna can't touch all of them," Rose says worriedly. "How will she keep track of who she's tested already?"

"That's what the rest of you are for," Anna jumps in. "His glamour is too strong for Rose and Kara to use their powers on him, but that alone is a sign of who he is. If Kara finds someone whose mind she can't read or Rose someone whose emotions she can't detect, it might be him, and I can check."

Nora's already shaking her head, but Anna protests. "It's the only way to find out who he is!"

"No. Out of the question," Nora says. "It's too dangerous."

"Ah, come on now, Nor." Roy slings an arm over his sister's shoulders. "We'll have her back." He snaps his fingers, and a tiny flame appears, hovering just above his palm. The house shudders, disgruntled.

Nora pushes his arm off, and the fire vanishes along with Roy's cheerful expression. "It's not just Anna," she says. "We'll be putting everyone at the party at risk."

Kara leans over her knees to look Nora in the eye. "We don't have a choice. Fin's coming no matter what."

Rose stares distantly out the library windows. "The trees can feel it."

"What if I left?" I ask, thinking of my plan in the motel parking lot. "Maybe he'd follow me. Then everyone here would be safe."

"Or maybe he'd send wraiths after you and still come here to try to destroy the Shield, and we'd be down a Raven," Kara replies with a shake of her head.

"And we're not sending you off again," Nora adds. Roy and Elaine both nod their agreement.

"Hmm," Gran says. Everyone turns to her, but she looks at me. "Only a weapon as powerful as the Saint Knives will be able to wound Fin, and only you can wield their magic. Without you, we have no hope of stopping Fin. You have to stay and defeat him."

Defeat him. Wound him. I realize now some part of me hadn't thought this through. Fin isn't a wraith. I can't just shake him free from his body with the Saint Knives for Max to glean. He's real, flesh and blood, no matter how messed up, and the only way to defeat him is to do the same thing he was trying to do to me: kill.

Why does that bother me so much? Fin murdered my parents, maybe my brother—he tried to kill me, and hurt Anna in the process. He has to be stopped.

But could I be the one to do it?

The wall sealing off my emotions begins to break. Anxiety slips through the cracks, threatening to make my head spin.

My first instinct is to hold my breath, to control the emotions until they fade. But then I catch Anna's concerned gaze, and I let the impulse go, allowing the feelings in.

"I'm not sure I'm ready for this," I say quietly.

"You don't have to be," she whispers. "You're not doing it alone."

Hearing those words is like unsealing a vacuum, and I let them wash over me. She's right. I might be the one to face Fin in the end, but the others are here for me.

It's a strange feeling. It's been just me, my parents, and Liam for the last few months, and even before that, I'd never been great at making friends. But Anna said she'd help me see this through, and somehow, I know she won't back down. I have at least one person in my corner.

I can tell by the expressions on the faces of Roy, Elaine, Gran, and the twins that they're in, too, but they all wait for Nora. She has a look that my mother used to get whenever I tried something new, like riding a bike. As if she can't bear to watch me fall but knows there's nothing she can do.

Finally, Nora visibly relents. "All right."

I nod as the severity of the situation hits home. This isn't some training exercise with Elaine and Roy in the backyard; this is real. People's lives will be at stake. My life will be at stake, and I'll have to rely on every trick and ounce of magic I've learned to win.

"We can do this," I say. "All of us, together."

And when Anna smiles at me, I know I'm right.

CHAPTER 22

Colin

We spend the morning of the party helping with last-minute decorations, which simultaneously feels pointless in the face of what's to come tonight and keeps me from thinking too much about it. Most of the big things are already taken care of, but there are still a lot of smaller things to do, and everyone is pitching in, even Max, who changed the house's hat to a black pointed witch's hat.

We dodge a couple guests already dressed in their costumes for that night on our way to the kitchen. One wears a convincing vampire outfit, and their friend has on a werewolf costume that looks so similar to the one from Seamus's shop that I watch them until they're out of sight just in case.

We spot the Andrades in matching crow masks, and Dilara, Rose's girlfriend, has come as a garden of flowers. Even Alice, the witch from the motel, has joined us. She wears only a simple black masquerade mask, but her skin is spelled with beautiful glowing tattoos, from tiny autumn leaves tumbling down her arms to a cup of tea with rising steam in the shape of ghosts.

The kitchen is alive with activity and Irish music. Every counter has something on it, from fresh-baked pumpkin pies to homemade marshmallows shaped as skeletons and Irish knots. Nora and Roy buzz from spot to spot, each wearing an apron that's doing absolutely no good to protect their clothes. Rose stands by the island, pouring batter into pans.

Anna picks a cake off a plate and splits it in half, handing part to me. Delicious, orange-scented steam wafts out.

"It's a soul cake," she says. "Dilara spelled them to prevent possession for a night." She holds it up in a toast. "To not getting possessed."

I smile halfheartedly and hold up my half. "To tonight."

"Is something wrong?" Anna asks through a mouthful of cake.

I lean against the island. "I've just been thinking about Liam. It's been over two weeks, and if Fin is in the Otherworld, and Kaden is in Wick somewhere, where is he?"

"It is strange," Anna agrees, then winces. "Sorry. I know that's not helping."

Except in a way, it does. I'm tired of false promises, of coded words meant to make me feel better.

"Thanks for being honest," I say, and she blinks at me in surprise. "It helps, knowing the truth. I like facts. They keep me steady. And you never lie to me. That's more than I can say about a lot of people in my life."

An all-encompassing grin breaks across her face, and I dig into my cake, my nerves settling.

We spend the rest of the day completing chore after chore,

from decorating to showing late guests to rooms to assuring them that the rumors about the place being haunted aren't true. For the most part. Anna says there *is* a ghost in the attic that the house refuses to let Gran send on.

As the sun begins to set, the last of the chores winding down, Anna finds me where I'm carrying plates of cookies to the ballroom. She leads me outside, where Elaine is waiting by the Charger with Max.

I slow, looking between them uncertainly.

"I had an idea earlier," Anna says. "You said you like facts and answers, so I know not knowing what happened to Liam must be really hard for you. I thought . . . if you want . . . Well, Aunt Elaine can talk to spirits. If Liam . . . If he's gone, she might be able to contact him."

My instinct is to say yes right away, but I hesitate. This means getting an answer one way or another—and I'm not sure I can handle that right now. If I don't do this, then for all I know there's still a chance Liam might come back. But if Elaine contacts his spirit . . .

But I can't say no. Not knowing would be worse.

"Let's do it," I say.

We climb into the Charger as Elaine explains the process. "The easiest way for me to reach a spirit is to channel through something they spent a lot of time with. Anna said your brother worked on this car a lot, so it should work perfectly."

I run my hand along the steering wheel. "How will we know if . . ."

"If I contact him?" Elaine sets out a couple candles on the dashboard. "He'll manifest here in an incorporeal form, similar to the ghosts you saw when you first arrived."

She lights the two candles, then angles in her seat to face me. Anna hangs over the seat from the back, scratching Max's ears where he lies across my shoulders. His fur is warm and soft against the back of my neck, and I try to focus on that.

"Are you sure about this?" Anna asks. "You don't have to."

"I know," I say quietly. "But I need to."

Elaine places her hand over mine and closes her eyes. She mutters under her breath in Irish. The candle flames dance in an invisible wind, and the trees rustle. Max watches apprehensively, and I know he's ready to transform. I've learned enough by now to know that if Liam is dead, we won't know how he died or how angry a spirit he'll be, and with any séance, there's always the risk that more spirits will come through, especially on Samhain.

Elaine's voice rises. "Reveal yourself!" she commands.

The air in the car thickens. A tree outside groans. Max crouches down against my neck.

"Reveal yourself!" she says again. Then a third time, "Reveal yourself!"

The air between us splits like a lightning strike. There's a flicker of a pale hand, then one bright gray eye. The air grows hazy, spinning and rippling, revealing another piece of the spirit each way it turns: a bloodied shoulder. Torn clothes. A gash above his brow.

Then Liam's face appears, his eyes wild. His mouth is open in a silent scream. I reach for him, shouting his name, but my hands go straight through the misty substance.

It swirls away, re-forming outside the car. Liam blinks into existence, then out again like a faulty light. He's one step away from the car, then ten, then three, then right up against the metal, reaching for me.

I reach back, desperate to grab his hand, but Max lets out a loud hiss and Elaine pulls me away.

Liam's hand stays outstretched, his mouth open, and only a single word comes out: "Run."

Then he's gone.

"No!" I yell.

The candles burn out. The wind goes quiet.

We sit in silence in the car. My breathing won't slow, my heart hammering in time with my racing thoughts.

He'd been a spirit. A *spirit*.

My voice breaks when I say, "That's it then. He's . . . he's gone."

"Not necessarily," Elaine says, and my eyes snap to her. "I've never experienced a séance like that before. As much as I was pulling Liam's spirit here, it was as if he were pulling me back to wherever he is. There was so much force to him, far more than a spirit."

"What are you saying?" Anna asks as hope rises in my chest.

Her brow furrows with confusion. "I'm honestly not sure."

CHAPTER 23

Anna

We part ways to get ready, though not before I make sure Colin's okay to be alone. Aunt Elaine's séance raised more questions than it answered, and he looked so overwhelmed. Liam isn't even my brother and my heart is still in my throat, the images of his spirit flashing in my mind. But Colin had clung to Aunt Elaine's suspicion that Liam is alive, and I hadn't wanted to say anything that might change that.

I return to my room and take a shower. Diffusing my hair takes its usual half hour, but by the time I'm done, it's curlier than ever and I love it.

I end up deciding on an asymmetrical black dress with one sleeve down to the elbow. A thin Gothic lace traces the chest and hem. The pin-on cat tail blends perfectly with the material. A pair of soft black shoes finishes it all off.

For a moment I look at myself in the mirror, my stomach a jumble of knots in anticipation. There will be something much more dangerous than a wraith in the house tonight, and I'm supposed to find him. I want so badly to prove that my powers are useful, but I can't hide the fact that I'm scared.

I sense my mother in my doorway before I see her in the mirror. Her smile is gentle and knowing, and I'm in her arms before either of us can speak.

She rubs circles on my back. "You don't have to do this, Anna," she says softly. "We can find another way."

I'm already shaking my head before she finishes. "No, I can't. I . . . I have to."

I pull away and drop onto my bed. Nora joins me, her arm coming around my shoulders. I start to protest—I don't need a hug to fix *everything*—but it feels nice, so I let her do it.

"Why do you have to?" Nora asks.

I twist my blanket in my fingers, fighting the words into existence. I've never said them to her before. "Because I can be useful for more than chores and errands. My powers can be useful."

Saying it aloud unlocks something inside me. All this time, I thought helping Colin and stopping Fin would prove that my powers are worth something, but I've known all along they are: I just needed everyone else to see it too.

Now I know that I don't need that either. I helped Colin settle into Ravenfall. I connected the dots between him and Fin. I discovered what was wrong with Gran and helped save her in time to get to Colin.

And I'd done it all without my powers.

This whole time I thought I needed them to matter, but they're only a small part of me. I don't need magic to be useful, and I belong at Ravenfall no matter what my powers do.

"Oh, my love," Nora says, pulling me close. Tears well up in my eyes, and I let them go. Then I hear her sniff and look up to find her crying too. "I'm so, so sorry. I never realized that's how you felt."

I look away, ashamed to have made her feel bad. But she gently places a hand on my face, turning me to look at her.

"I kept you from the guests because I didn't want to burden you with responsibilities," she says. "I wanted to let you be a kid for as long as possible, and not force you to grow up fast, as I had to. I didn't want this place to consume your life the same way it consumed mine."

My tears slow, and I wipe my arm across my eyes. "What do you mean?"

Nora's expression softens. "Ravenfall is a wonderful, wonderful place, but it was never my dream to run it. I've thought of myself as a prisoner for so long that I became one. But I should never have assumed that you'd want the same things as I did, and for that, I'm sorry."

She squeezes my hand. "Psychometry is a rare and wonderful gift, Anna, and I'm so happy it chose you. Give it a chance. It is a gift that will grow with time."

I nod, comforted by the surety in her voice and the knowledge that my mother has never lied to me. My hands tangle up in the blanket, the wool scratchy against my palms, yet comforting in its familiarity. This is my blanket, my bed, my house. I am safe here, no matter what we face tomorrow.

"It is my dream, though," I tell her. "I want to run Ravenfall one day."

A smile breaks slowly across her face. "I couldn't think of a better person to fill my shoes."

Hearing her say that is like the first sip of hot chocolate on a cold night, filling me with warmth and comfort I didn't know I needed. I should have told Nora how I felt earlier instead of trying to handle it all on my own.

Bolstered, I set my blanket aside. "I'm ready."

She pulls me close once more. "I know you are."

She kisses me on the head and stands just as the twins arrive, their makeup box in tow. They wear identical red and black dresses with sweetheart necklines and unevenly cut hems, their masks and jewelry matching. Rose forwent her wings once we'd realized everyone needed to be able to move around the crowd, but I have a feeling she'll find another chance to wear them.

Nora touches them each on the shoulder as she leaves.

"Oh," Rose says, looking about the room at something only she can see. "This feels nice."

Kara assesses me with a quirk of her lips and says, "Of course you belong here. The house wouldn't want anyone else."

The house rumbles its agreement, and I grin.

The twins buzz around me, applying different things with brushes. Normally I don't wear makeup—I always forget and touch my face—but every year I let them do it on Samhain as part of my costume.

"Nothing too ridiculous," I warn them.

"Never," they agree together.

When they finish, I have no choice but to grudgingly admit they've done a good job. They always do. Shadowy eyes and perfectly drawn whiskers. The cat mask will cover most of it, but at least I'll look great when I take it off.

"Yeah you will," Kara says.

I grab the mask from the bed and fix it carefully on my face.

I love parties, especially on Samhain, but by the end of them I'm usually exhausted and have seen far too many people die.

Most of them are peaceful, people passing away in hospitals or asleep in their beds, but every once in a while, there's a car crash or an accident that sears itself in my mind. All those images and, worse, the emotions, add up.

But tonight, I feel as though I can face it.

"Ready?" Kara asks, offering me her arm. The buzz of the growing crowd downstairs is already filtering up to my room.

Rose holds out her arm, too, and I step between them, taking both. "Ready," she says.

"Not even close," I reply with a grin.

CHAPTER 24

Colin

The ballroom is in top form tonight. I've never seen Halloween decorations look so elegant. Orange paper lanterns hang from the ceiling among the teardrop lights, and the tables are draped with shimmering cloths. Jack-o'-lanterns with intricate designs sit next to autumn wreaths and red apples. Scattered among the tables and the lights above are glass figurines in the shapes of bats, cats, and other magical creatures I now recognize: kelpies and black dogs, merrows and selkies, and even a Jabberwocky, though the house gave it the worst spot in the room.

My favorite, though, is Max, who sits still as a statue until someone approaches saying how lifelike he looks before lunging.

It's almost enough to distract me from what's coming. Almost.

We'd gathered that morning to review the plan: once Fin arrived, Kara and Rose would scan the crowd with their powers, looking for dead spots. Then Anna would approach and touch each person nearby. If she found Fin, she would signal Gran or Nora, who would be watching her, and then get to safety.

Meanwhile, Roy, Elaine, and I would be patrolling the crowd, looking for signs of wraiths and ready to step in if anyone looked to be in danger.

Dilara had supplied the partygoers with rowanberry bracelets from the Wicked Orchid, and almost everyone wore one. She'd also set up bundles of berries around the house to help weaken spirits, while Alice had offered to maintain a protection spell on the ballroom to prevent magical attacks.

If all went according to plan, I'd confront Fin once we found him, and the others would evacuate the ballroom.

Then all I had to do was win.

Max has just spooked an older couple coming down from their room, and we're both laughing when Anna and the twins enter, looking fantastic.

"Yes, I'd say we look fabulous as well," says Kara as they reach the base of the stairs.

"Thank you for saying so," says Rose, and my cheeks flush.

The twins laugh and slip their arms from Anna's, drifting toward where Dilara is waving at them in the crowd.

Anna clasps her hands before her. "You look great too," she says. "Though I think there's a bit of blood on your shoulder."

I check my shoulder before I can stop myself. It's clean. This isn't even my suit, but an old one of Roy's, and his husband, Jamie, spent the entire evening fitting it to my size. The silver vest and black dress shirt are also his.

Anna laughs, and I grin, offering her my arm. She slips hers through mine and we both pause as Max leaps onto my shoulders.

"Time to stop an ancient Irish god from destroying the fabric of the universe." She says it jokingly, but I can feel the tenseness of her arm against mine.

I squeeze it reassuringly. "No big deal."

We start through the house, weaving between people in costumes and tables of snacks. Neither of us makes it past one without snagging a chocolate pumpkin or spiced cookie. Irish music fills the room, light and quick. The tables have been moved to the side, leaving a dance floor open by the base of the stairs. The entire place is filled with masked faces.

Anna holds tighter to my arm and our eyes meet. She doesn't say anything, but the reassurance behind them is clear.

"There you two are!" Elaine's voice rings out over the clamor. She slips nimbly between two guests dressed as faeries to join us. Her costume reflects tonight's plans, resembling a superhero in all black leather and a simple black mask, complete with a wooden staff for fighting.

"Has anyone noticed anything yet?" I ask, keeping my attention on the crowd.

"Not yet," Elaine replies. "Gran says we'll know when he's here. The whole party will, even if they don't know what they're sensing."

I feel Anna relax beside me and I let out a breath. Although I'm relieved, the idea of waiting longer makes my insides squirm.

"We should enjoy the party while we can, then." Anna pulls me into the throng.

I've never seen someone navigate a crowd so expertly. Anna moves with the flexibility of a snake, winding through people until we reach the other side and step out onto the porch.

The back of the house looks as magnificent as the rest. There are even more lights and paper lanterns out here, scattered throughout the grass and hanging from the deck railing. There are bonfires going in several of the pits off to the side, and Anna leads me toward them.

"Is there food in this direction?" I ask, noting a table with scraps of paper and pens on the edge of the largest pit. There's another one on the other side that looks as if it might have something edible. Max groans as if to second my question.

"I hope so."

After filling plates with food, we sit down at the table with the paper and pens and slide our masks off to eat.

"You write something you want to be rid of on the paper, like an old habit, and then you drop it in the fire," Anna explains as she balances her plate in one hand and picks up a pen with the other. "It disappears in the flames."

"Can I do more than one?" I ask. When she's forced to look at me to check if I'm joking, I can't hold back a smile. "One day you'll accept that I can be funny too," I tell her, setting down my plate to pick up a pen and slip of paper.

Anna snorts quietly and uses her body to shield her paper from view. "I think we need to work on your definition of funny first."

"Right. I'll just put 'bad jokes' down on here, then." This time she actually laughs.

It takes me a moment to decide what to write down. Finally I scribble *Loneliness* down on the paper and fold it in half. We toss the pieces into the fire, watching and eating our food as the flames grab hold and turn the notes to ash.

CHAPTER 25

Anna

The tradition of throwing papers into the bonfire is my favorite. Despite how simple it seems to write something down and toss it into the flames, the action feels big. It's similar to making a New Year's resolution, but watching the paper burn is far more satisfying than making a promise to myself. This is like making a promise to something bigger than me instead.

I write a single word on mine: *Loneliness.* Then I toss it in the fire.

"I suppose we can't tell each other what we wrote?" Colin asks. The firelight makes his pale skin glow.

I grin. "Nope."

A couple of other guests toss papers into the fire, lingering to watch them burn before drifting back to the main party. The music has shifted from the liveliness of before to something slower, haunting and beautiful. It drifts like a river out of the house and down to where we stand.

I sway to it, and catch Max doing the same at Colin's side. His fingers twitch as if he wants to join, but he only wraps his arms around his stomach.

"Come on," I say. "One dance before we take on the King of the Dead?"

A smile breaks across his face, and he starts shifting his weight. An array of high, ghostly voices join the song, singing in Irish. I know the trio of witches singing—Alice and her friends. Their voices are like a siren's song; I can listen forever. I close my eyes, focusing on the sound of the music, letting it flow in and through me, filling me up with their power.

The song begins to pick up pace and I snatch both of Colin's hands, spinning us in circles across the grass. We dance around paper lanterns and carved pumpkins, Max weaving between our feet. We laugh, and with each step my body grows lighter, as if I'm slowly turning into nothing but air. The world becomes a blur of color and light and sound, wrapping us in a protective cocoon, and for that moment, everything is perfect.

Then the music reaches its peak, and the lightness is crushed by an overwhelming sense of cold and despair.

I gasp, my eyes flying open. Colin tenses. The song comes to an end and we both fall still. My back is toward the house and a presence I don't want to face. Footsteps sound behind me and I turn.

"He's here," says Rose with a shiver, her arms wrapped about her chest.

I swallow hard, my skin prickling with goose bumps. Rubbing them does nothing; the chill is from the inside.

I don't want to leave the field, wishing for a second that if I don't move, the moment won't have to end. We won't have to do this.

"Okay," I say finally. "Let's go."

The three of us cross the field to the porch. Throughout the rest of the house, the party continues unchanged. For the out-of-town guests, this is just another celebration. They have no idea what lurks in their midst. Only the locals have sensed the change in the air, Alice among them. She clutches a pale gold crystal in her hand, the light pulsating as she begins her protection spell with the help of her friends.

Gran, Nora, Kara, Aunt Elaine, and Uncle Roy find us before we find them, Uncle Roy pulling Jamie after him by the hand. They're dressed in matching sailor costumes, and before Uncle Roy reaches us, he says something quietly to Jamie and kisses him on the cheek. Worry lines his face, but he lets Uncle Roy go as the crowd swallows him up.

Dilara arrives at Rose's side and slides their hands together. "We'll take the left," Dilara says.

Kara nods. "I'm on the right."

They stand back-to-back, their gazes scanning opposite sides of the crowd, looking for people who their powers can't reach.

Gran and Nora join me. They won't stay too close, or else someone may suspect something's happening, but they'll keep an eye on me so I can signal them when I find Fin.

Aunt Elaine can barely stand still. Colin is antsy, too, shifting his weight from side to side, but Uncle Roy stands steady as a mountain.

"Right," Aunt Elaine says. "While this is all happening, keep in mind he's after you, too, Colin."

"Be careful," Nora warns us all, before Uncle Roy and Aunt Elaine disperse into the crowd to patrol. Colin stays with us to watch our backs.

We stand tensely side by side, two coiled springs, while the twins work. Rose presses a hand to her head. "There are so many more spots than I'd have imagined."

Kara grimaces. "Exactly *who* did we invite this year?"

"These are all too small," Rose mutters. "Too small . . ."

Max joins us as they search. I'm starting to regret ever eating anything as my stomach roils with anticipation, my fingers twitching at my sides.

"There." Rose raises the hand clasped with Dilara's to point toward the stairs at the right of the ballroom. "Close to the edge of the crowd. Someone over there is creating a very large dead spot."

Colin shoots forward like a runner from his starting block and I move after him, catching him by the arm and dragging him to a halt. "You can't just run in there! Fin wants you, not me, and I need to find him first. That's the plan."

"I know the plan!" Colin's jaw tightens. "But if it's him, I can end this myself. I don't want to put you in the middle of this."

"It might not even be him. We're sticking to the plan. Together, remember?" I squeeze his shoulder and step past him, slipping my mask over my face. "Stay back and keep an eye on Nora and Gran while you're patrolling. I'll signal them when I find him."

I don't give Colin the chance to argue before I dive into the crowd. Dodging people has become one of my greatest skills, but I still bump into the occasional person without meaning to. Thankfully none of them trigger any visions, but I slow down as I approach the area Rose indicated just in case.

I find a patch of space and scan the crowd. Masks, masks, and more masks stare back at me.

Drawing a deep breath, I start "accidentally" brushing and

bumping into people. I avoid women and children, and anyone who looks too tall or too short to match what I saw of Fin. After eliminating people whose body type differs drastically or who has red or blond hair, I'm down to a decent number, though the two I've touched so far were duds.

Stepping up beside a man with a devil's mask on, I let my hand graze his. Instantly the spot goes cold as I'm swept into a vision.

I'm sitting in a hard wooden chair. The walls are painted a sickly white, and the beep of hospital machines punctuates the background.

My mother's face is peaceful in sleep. Her gnarled hand is clasped in mine, and I hold it close as the beeping slows, then stops.

I wobble briefly but maintain my balance as my head clears. The sadness lingers, but I push it away.

So the devil is a dud. That leaves a man with a black and forest-green masquerade mask, who I can't get a good look at, and another with a wolf's mask that covers even his eyes with thin material. There was a third, but I can't find him.

I maneuver behind the man with the wolf mask and tense when I brush him with my fingers. Nothing. Except he does turn, giving me a suspicious look.

"Sorry," I say, stepping around him to find the next man. Someone grabs my arm, sending tendrils of ice racing up my veins. I try to pull away, but the vision gets to me first.

It's unlike anything I've ever seen.

The clash of steel. The flash of Saint Knives. Blood, screaming. My body is exhausted and in pain, but I don't stop fighting. I can't stop fighting.

Bodies drop around me. The war goes on.

The scene changes, flashing to another vision, another death.

The guard's body drops to the ground with a thud, and I pull my knife free.

The visions continue in quick succession. There's a woman

with red-painted lips and pointed ears. A selkie halfway through transforming. A boy barely older than Rose.

Image after image flashes, death after death, until one surges to the top, stronger than all the others.

I stand motionless beside a chair, listening to the man tied to it refuse my request. He won't tell me where the other Ravens are. He is a waste of my precious time. His wife's life force will only sustain me on this side for so long; I will need his to last longer.

My hand closes around his throat. I draw his life from him in a rush of heady power.

Then the motel room door flies open. Two boys enter, and Kaden tackles the youngest. The older comes for me.

My body is ragged and slow. The older boy puts a knife in my ribs. I leap for the window, but not before another knife lodges in my back. I must return to the Otherworld before my energy fades.

My knees threaten to buckle as the vision vanishes. The cold doesn't recede from where Fin is touching me; it only grows. He stares down at me, his emerald eyes made bolder by the black and green mask.

His voice is ancient when he speaks. "You should never have gotten involved."

CHAPTER 26

Colin

I should never have let Anna go off alone, plan or not.

It's hard to keep track of her with all the people, most of whom are wearing black, and I can tell Gran and Nora are having just as much trouble. More than once I shove people out of the way to make sure that I keep her in sight, and they're not happy when I don't stop to apologize.

Anna reaches for a man in a devil's mask. Her entire body goes rigid. Already I'm imagining the feel of my Saint Knives, leaning forward to slip through the crowd. But before I can even take a step, Anna recovers and moves on.

"Sweet blades, dude!" Someone claps me on the back and moves on. I stare down at the Saint Knives in my hands. It takes me a moment to force my tight grip to relax.

Then the knives begin to sing.

My head jerks up. Kaden stands directly ahead of me. The knives cry louder, but the sound is overcome by the music and voices.

The smile on Kaden's lips sets fire to my skin and I long to knock it off, until I realize why he's smiling. I move to the side, looking around him, but I can't see her. Kaden was just a distraction.

Anna is gone.

Nora pushes through the crowd to where she was last, pale with fear. "Did you see where she went?"

I shake my head. Our plan is already falling apart. Anna must have found Fin, and now they're both missing.

Kaden laughs and sets off toward the rear stairs. I go after him, hoping he'll lead me to Fin and Anna, but Kaden reaches the stairs while I'm still fighting through the crowd. By the time I hit the bottom step, he's already disappeared through the double doors at the top.

Max joins me at the top, and we barrel around the corner to find Kaden waiting in the hallway. He bolts, and we follow. Where is he leading me? The hallway is lined with glass and broken pictures, doors all along it flung open, as if the house went wild.

We duck through open doors and down corridors, moving deeper into the maze of the house. As we curve around another corner, we reach a dead end, and Kaden whirls to face me.

He clasps his hands behind his back, an inhuman smile on his lips.

"No more running," I say. "We're ending this now."

"But you were being such a good boy," he mocks.

I know Kaden is just a distraction, but I'm also sure he knows where Anna is. I look to Max, but he's already shifting, his body turning translucent as he darts through the nearest wall to look for her.

"Where is she? Where's Fin?" I keep one knife fully palmed but prepare the other to throw.

Kaden's smirk only grows. "Finally found his name, have you? Took you all long enough." His laugh sounds like something dying.

I lunge for him.

CHAPTER 27

Anna

I break Fin's hold on my wrist and take off. There's no choice but to go for the stairs; there are too many people to fight through any other direction. I can feel him following me, and I pray that the others are watching. I have a few tricks here and there, but I can't take on someone this strong.

Then again, I should have known better than to think it would be a fair fight.

As I sail down the hall, the house shudders. Doors fly open in my wake, forcing Fin to dodge from side to side. Picture frames shoot from the walls, their glass shattering when they slam into him, but he doesn't slow.

What does he want with me?

I make my way to the front of the house and up to the third floor. When Fin reaches the stairs, they begin to splinter beneath his weight. He navigates them with the grace of a cat, and I force myself to stop looking back; it's only slowing me down.

My throat burns as I reach the fourth floor, shooting down the nearest hallway. I'm running out of house, and Fin isn't relenting. I head for the only room I know might have a weapon: Roy's. Fin stays in close pursuit, and I have the distinct feeling of being toyed with, like a cat chasing a mouse. Can he catch me if he wants to?

Roy's door flies open before I reach it and slams shut behind me, locking. There's a safe in the corner of his room. The lock spins to the correct numbers and the door pops open. Inside sits his weapons collection: throwing knives, daggers, a pair of long-swords, even an ax.

They float out, filling the space between me and the door.

Something strikes the door. It groans, the hinges threatening to give. Sweat glistens on my skin, dampening my palms. I retreat toward the wall, tearing off my mask as the door crashes to the ground.

The house sends every last one of Roy's weapons flying at Fin.

He sweeps his hand across his body, deflecting them into the walls and out the windows. They quiver where they've struck, the house struggling to regain control of them.

My heart races wildly. I hadn't doubted Fin's power, but if he's telekinetic, then he's truly strong. Gran is the only person I've ever known with that power, and when it comes to her magic, she's as much a mystery to me as the man before me.

Fin's lips form the slightest of smiles. He raises a hand and I flinch, but he only removes his masquerade mask. At first his face is blurred, and I can't get a hold on any single feature. But the harder I stare, the more it clears, until I can truly see him.

His features are sharp like a hawk's, his skin as pale as Colin's, with eyelashes so dark they create a black rim around his emerald eyes. He has an ethereal beauty that's sharp enough to cut, and he looks exactly as he did in my Radharc vision—as though not a single day has gone by since that ancient battle.

"Why are you doing this?" I ask.

By now it's clear that something stopped the others from following me, but I'm sure the house will lead them to me soon. The longer I delay, the better chance I have.

Fin plays with the edge of the mask, turning it in circles with slow, deliberate movements. "My people have suffered long in the darkness and cold of the Otherworld," he replies. "I will see them freed, and I will see revenge upon those who condemned us to that place."

"That was hundreds of years ago! Whoever's responsible for that is long dead."

He tilts his head to the side, slow and birdlike. "But their descendants yet live." He tosses the mask to the ground and steps toward me. I retreat, the wall pressing into me from behind. He stops with only a few feet between us. The brilliant green of his eyes is flecked with bits of black now. "Your family, my dear Miss Ballinkay, are the descendants of our enemies. And I will see them removed from this earth."

The black spreads fully across his irises, and my heart plummets to my stomach.

Everything happens so fast. Fin lifts a hand, pressing me against the wall with his telekinesis. An invisible pressure crashes down on my throat, cutting off the air. The house shudders. Then a luminous form barrels through me, sending a chill streaking along every inch of my body. It slams into Fin, knocking him to the ground.

Gasping, I fight to regain my breath as Max solidifies before me. His face says it all: *Run!*

I skirt around Fin and shoot out the door, Max in my wake.

I have to find Colin.

CHAPTER 28

Colin

K aden is as quick as I expect him to be, but this time I'm quicker. It's all he can do to parry my blows. Our blades clash and the song of the Saint Knives fills the hall. Kaden hardly looks bothered by it.

When I clang them together, he only grins. I hit them again, and his form shifts like that day on the bridge, going from human to wraith in a flicker.

"My soul has absorbed my host's," he says through rows of needle teeth. "All that sound does is annoy me."

I lower the knives. "That's fine. I'd rather defeat you myself."

"Why bother?" He lifts his blade. "Everyone you care for is dead. Your parents. Your brother. Even the little psychic."

Everything in me goes cold. Kaden takes the opportunity, lunging for me. His knife clips my bicep and I grit my teeth, barreling straight back at him.

He deflects my first strike, but I follow through with my foot and catch him in the ribs, sending him stumbling. Had he just said that to put me off guard? My heart feels like it's everywhere, drumming against my skin, urging me to hurry.

Kaden regains himself and flips a blade at my chest. I strike it from the air and release one of my own in the same movement. It buries in Kaden's shoulder. He howls, the arm going limp, and I summon my knife back to my hand.

"If he's hurt her . . ." I advance on the injured wraith. Kaden retreats, one clawed hand clasped on his shoulder, silver blood snaking between his fingers. "I'll make you wish you had never merged with that man's soul." Kaden's back hits a wall, his coal-black eyes wide. "And then I will kill you, and Fin, and any other monster who gets in my way."

Kaden holds up his bloodstained claws, cringing against the wall. "I haven't done anything to her." His words tumble out in a torrent. "My lord took her. I don't know why. I don't know what he wants with her. She's probably fine. He wants her for bait. That's all."

The house shakes violently. Screams erupt from downstairs, distant and ghostly. Reflexively, I turn to look. I feel Kaden move, my body already responding. As he lunges, claws outstretched for my throat, I turn, catching him through the chest with the blade.

His body strikes the ground, then turns to silver dust, disappearing into the floorboards.

"Colin!"

I whirl at Anna's voice. She's sprinting toward me, Max at her side. I let my blades vanish as she flings her arms around me. I catch her and relief swallows me whole.

The house rocks again and we both tense, drawing apart. The commotion from downstairs is still wafting up through the floor, a reminder that this isn't over.

"Where's Fin?" I ask as Anna lets go.

"Right behind me."

My hot skin itches and I shift to stand in front of her as Fin appears around the corner. He walks so leisurely you'd think he was just out for a stroll.

"The two of you are making this unnecessarily difficult," he says, slowing to a halt. It's odd seeing his face clearly. He has the sharp lines and unyielding posture of a king, just as he did in my vision, and he's dressed the part as well. Somehow his leather and satin clothing is both suited to regality and fighting.

"Right. We'll just stand here and let you kill us, then." Anna's hands are curled into fists. I can see the fear beneath her anger, her swift breathing and the sweat glistening on her skin.

Fin slides his hands from his pockets. His face is impassive, as if this is simply a chore that needs taking care of.

My Saint Knives materialize in my hands. Fin assesses the blades, his bright eyes slowly darkening as the pupils expand. "You misunderstand," he growls. "It's only one of you I want dead."

He moves first, faster than Kaden ever was. The distance between us vanishes as he strikes out, nearly catching me on the chin. Anna retreats as I slash my knives at Fin's chest, but he slips away with ease.

Back and forth we go until Fin catches my wrist, wringing it. Pain erupts up my forearm, forcing me to drop the knife. Fin's fist connects with the side of my face, and he twists my wrist harder. I cry out, sinking to my knees.

Fire rips through my veins, pain and anger unrelenting. Fin stares down at me, his features collected and calm. For an impossibly drawn-out moment, something resonates between us. It feels similar to the link I have with my journal: like magic, but as though *I'm* the journal and Fin is reaching *into me* and drawing something out.

Then Fin's eyes flare. A knife flies past me, aimed at his heart. He sweeps out a hand, sending it into the wall beside us. I strike out with my other knife, catching him across the chest with a thin slice as he leaps back.

When he lands, the floor crumbles underneath him.

CHAPTER 29

Anna

I knew that Fin would deflect the blade I threw, but I only needed to distract him. The house takes care of the rest. As Fin disappears to the floor below, I seize Colin's arm. "We need to get back to the others!"

We take off down the hall, returning to the staircase and down to the ballroom. We enter into chaos. Screams echo as spirits flood the room, more than I've ever seen, but the real threat is the wraiths.

There are way more than we expected, and my family is overwhelmed.

Aunt Elaine and Uncle Roy face a wraith together. Gran has two pinned telekinetically to the high ceiling. With a flick of her wrist, they crash to the floor. Alice is still casting her protection spell as the guests flee, and the spirits rebound off invisible shields of light when they get too close to people. Dilara has taken over the singing ivy, manipulating it to wrap around the ankles of wraiths, and Mr. and Mrs. Andrade are helping to direct guests to safety.

Spirits nearly overrun the open space, creating a sea of light. Max weaves through them, gleaning them as fast as he can. But as he clears them away, they reappear twice as quickly. All around us the house creaks and groans.

We thought we could keep the guests safe; we were wrong.

"Come on! Let's lead Fin outside, away from the guests." I sprint down the stairs and plunge into the fray of souls. The cold enters my body in a rush, slowing me down, but the soul cakes keep us safe from possession. Still, fighting through the spirits is like wading through water. We break through on the other side, panting heavily and chilled to the bone.

The doors to the porch are off their hinges, their glass shattered. It crunches underfoot as we run outside and down the stairs to the field.

The Shield stretches out before us as far as the eye can see in either direction and high into the clouds.

It appears every Samhain, visible to those with magic, but I've never seen it in such a bad state. Normally alight with a golden glow bright enough to illuminate Ravenfall, it's now a pale, sickly yellow that pulsates like a fading heartbeat. Thin black cracks spiderweb across it, resembling the poison that had spread up Gran's arm, and pieces flake away, dispersing into nothing.

Even with Colin still alive, Fin's plan is working. The Shield is dying.

Rose and Kara stand before it, their hands pressed against the golden light. They're channeling their magic into it, trying to strengthen it.

"I can feel the Shield," says Colin as we slow beside it. "I feel stronger here."

"You're a channel for it." I stand with my hands on my knees, breathing hard. "It will help you, so long as it can."

Which from the looks of it isn't much longer.

Movement around the front of the house draws my eye and I straighten. "There."

Fin approaches us, his previously well-manicured clothing now ripped and dusted. The wound Colin dealt to his chest is barely visible, and blood stains his leg.

"Draw on the Shield!" I shout to Colin as I thrust my hands against it, adding my strength. The Shield welcomes it, pulling my magic and energy from me in a steady stream.

A slow smile spreads across Fin's lips. "Yes, please do. The more you draw from it the weaker it will grow. These children's powers will only sustain it for so long."

Colin looks at me and I nod. There's no other way. He has to defeat Fin before we run out of energy and the Shield grows weak enough for him to break. I don't want to think what kind of creatures wait on the other side—and then suddenly I don't have to.

The surface of the Shield clears, and I glimpse rows of spirits and creatures on the other side, each more gruesome-looking than the last. I bite back a scream. Some look just like people, their faces pale and ghostly in the Shield's light. Others might have been people—once. Creatures with long fangs rake curving claws down the Shield's edge; spirits with peeling skin and wide, bloodshot eyes; shapes that are more shadow and claws than person, all waiting to descend the moment Fin destroys the Shield.

"How ironic it is that my own descendant guards my prison," Fin says. "Clever, these psychics, and very cruel."

"Enough stalling." Colin lunges forward, faster than before. It catches Fin off guard and Colin lands a quick combination on his jaw and stomach, forcing him back. Fin counters, but Colin leaps away. Those were blows that would have flattened a normal man, but Fin hardly looks fazed.

Fin thrusts out a hand. At first, I think nothing happened, but then I see Colin straining, every muscle in his body tightening. Fin is trying to control him telekinetically.

"More!" I shout to Rose and Kara, pouring my energy into the Shield. It brightens and Colin gasps, his movements returning to normal speed. He summons a knife and sends it flying. Fin brushes out his hand, meaning to deflect it, but the blade doesn't stop and buries in his shoulder.

He hisses, the first real sign of emotion cracking his stoic expression. His telekinesis didn't work on the Saint Knife.

"Hurry, Colin!" I can feel myself waning. Kara has already collapsed against the Shield, her ragged breathing wracking her entire body.

The Shield fades more, the cracks growing larger.

Fin rips the knife out of his shoulder, inspecting it. "I'd forgotten," he mutters. Then the knife vanishes, reappearing in Colin's hand.

"Do you really mean to kill me?" Fin presses his fingers against the wound without reaction. "I am, after all, the only family you have left."

Colin's hands tighten around the knives. "I think you've been trapped in hell too long."

A wicked smile spreads across Fin's face. "Not hell, my dear boy, but a forever in-between full of the creatures that have spawned every horror story across time. Hell would be paradise in comparison." He pulls his hand away from the wound, spreading the blood across his fingers as if testing its texture.

"But no matter." His voice is a gust of wind. "All will be right soon enough."

My eyes narrow, my vision blurring with my draining energy. There's something off about his face.

My knees buckle and I collapse to the grass. Fin's smile spreads wider as Colin runs toward me, but I keep staring at Fin. Something isn't right.

Colin drops beside me, but I can't feel his hands as he shakes me. He tries to pull me from the Shield, but it won't let me go. It feeds off my strength without mercy, desperate to keep itself alive. A distant thud behind me tells me Rose has fallen too.

Still I stare at Fin, my mind slow as dripping honey, and finally I see it. His face. It's all glamour. The illusion falls away, revealing rotted gray skin and sinew, faded bone and decaying flesh.

Fin went into the Otherworld a living being and emerged in the same body. An ancient, decaying body.

"Anna!" Colin's voice is distant.

I feel my lips moving, feel myself speaking words in a quiet whisper. "Fin's still in his original body. It's . . . a glamour. A . . ." Darkness creeps in at the edges of my vision, and in the back of my mind I'm vaguely aware that the house has gone silent.

CHAPTER 30

Colin

Anna's voice fades and her body goes limp as the Shield finally releases her. I lay her gently on the ground and feel for her pulse. Her heartbeat is faint, but it's there. Her body is unimaginably cold, and I quickly undo my vest, laying it over her. She needs more than that, but the Shield is so weak.

We're running out of time.

Cracks reach across the Shield's entire surface now, resembling glass about to shatter. As its glow continues to fade, shapes grow more visible on the other side. Dark, churning images like clouds of black smoke, twisting as if in pain. Animalistic roars mix with screams, the sounds barreling into the Shield and bouncing back, dulled. A dark, shadowy figure reaches out for me, its eyes bright gray.

I face Fin, both knives in hand. Anna's words echo in my head. Fin's still in his original body. Unlike his people, who became spirits and possessed new people, his body has survived.

Anna told me that as a warning. But a warning of what?

Fin closes the distance between us. I try to strike but he leaps aside as if pulled by a string. I can't match his speed. He begins to laugh, the darkness engulfing his eyes. Then he's before me, wrenching a knife out of my hand with a twist of my injured wrist. I barely register the pain before he drives his fist into my stomach, knocking the air from my lungs.

My knees buckle, hitting the ground hard. I struggle to breathe. Fin looms over me, his eyes completely black. As he reaches for my throat, the ground shudders. Fin jerks his head up just in time to dodge a massive black tail. A harsh bellow follows it, full of pain and anger.

"Max," I whisper, clutching my stomach. The Jabberwocky's tail encircles me, holding firm. His fur is wild, splayed in all directions with something wet and dripping. Blood. He's covered in it, his body peppered with wounds of his own from the wraith battles. Silver light spills through them, dispersing like mist in sunlight, and his chest rises and falls in ragged heaves.

Fin laughs, my view of him blurring as my head begins to feel light. He sounds maniacal, the last remnants of his ancient aura quickly disappearing.

"Your pet Jabberwocky can't defeat me alone," he says. "He's half dead himself."

Max tenses. When had I started leaning against him so heavily? There's a scraping sound behind me. Anna moves, her body twitching in her sleep.

"No," she whispers. "Max, no." She's fading fast; I can feel it. I press my hands into the grass for balance. The cold ground is the only thing I can feel besides the dull pain in my stomach. Everything else has gone numb.

Max steps forward, his tail unwinding from around me. His

body ripples, turning translucent. Anna mutters incoherently—or perhaps I just can't hear through the growing numbness.

There's a sharp hiss, and I manage to raise my head in time to see Max pull one clawed hand from his chest, a beating, glowing heart of energy pumping in his palm. Deep inside, something tells me to stop him. But it's such a quiet voice. So quiet it can't compete with the one telling me to lie down and sleep.

Max crushes the beating heart.

Pure energy explodes from his body. It's as if his luminosity has separated from him. His physical body collapses to the ground, shrinking into cat form. The silver energy spreads, breaking apart into separate streams. It dives into Kara and Rose, then Anna. She gasps, bolting upright. The last of it strikes me in the chest, knocking me back.

"No!" Anna's scream pierces me as powerfully as the energy, which drives through every inch of my body. Everything comes alive again. The pain flares, my skin tingles and burns, my muscles scream. Then all at once it goes quiet, and I feel more powerful than ever.

The smile is gone from Fin's face when I sit up. But it isn't him I care about. It's the limp black form in the grass beside me.

"Max?" I reach for him. He's already cold.

Anna drops beside him, her cheeks flushed and wet with tears. She wraps him up, drawing him close to her chest. "The Shield," she whispers, her voice breaking.

The Shield is more jagged lines than solid pieces now, and the things on the other side strain against it. I rise to my feet, flexing my fingers. Max's energy courses through me, and on my chest the trinity tattoo glows silver. It pulses with the growing anger inside me. Fin has taken yet another person I love from me.

Fin shoots forward, and I meet his knife with mine. He's still quick, but I'm equally as fast. I swipe at his stomach. He leaps away but I close the distance.

Fin merely smiles. "We can do this all night," he says. "I'm in no rush."

He's right. The Shield is one strike away from shattering, the last of its glow fading, and my body is weakening. Max's energy has helped, but it isn't enough to defeat Fin.

I can't let him sacrifice himself for nothing.

Fin's next blow takes the air out of my lungs. I clutch at my stomach, and his fist catches the side of my face. My vision blurs, and I stumble. I can barely hold myself upright.

A hand closes around my throat. That feeling from the hallway when Fin grabbed me returns. It feels like being drawn in, like a rope pulling me out, out, out . . . and something new takes its place.

My toes go numb, and then my feet, as gradually I lose control of my own body. Is this how my parents felt when Fin absorbed their life force? Is he using me as he used them?

Fin's voice is suddenly in my head, in my heart, in every part of me. "Imagine my surprise when you burst into that motel room. Your whole family may have been my descendants, but only you inherited a sliver of my power. Only you have the strength to contain me."

Contain. My tired mind spins around the word. *Contain.*

Anna's warning from earlier clicks into place: Fin's still in his original body—a body that's *decomposing*. He needs a new one.

Fin was never trying to kill me: he's trying to *possess* me!

As if the glamour had only been waiting for me to understand, it fades away, revealing rotting flesh stretched thin over torn muscle and bits of bone glaring white among the red.

I struggle in his grip, desperate to get away, but his laughter resounds inside my head. "It's too late, little Raven. Your body will be mine. I will be young and strong, and with your magic I will destroy what remains of this barrier and release my people so that they, too, can find new bodies."

My strength runs out, and I go limp in his grip. He chuckles quietly. "It's over."

A light shimmers at my side. A feeling unlike any other runs through me: warmth and sunlight, the windows open on a long highway, the scent of a forest after it rains. Like the link drawing me to Fin, it stretches between me and the person taking shape at my side as they step from the darkness.

Fin's hold on me breaks, and all at once feeling comes rushing back into my body. Hands find my arms and draw me to my feet, steadying me.

Liam.

My brother stands beside me. A little worse for wear with a gash above his eye and another through the shoulder of his leather jacket, but here. Solid.

I reach out quivering fingers to touch him, brushing real flesh.

"Yes," he agrees with Fin. "It is." He meets my gaze with a smile that engulfs his tired face.

I stare at him, barely daring to breathe. He's here. He's alive. He's— *"How?"* I breathe.

"I followed Fin into the Otherworld," Liam explains with an apologetic grimace. He indicates his shoulder. "He thought he'd killed me, but I survived. His attack broke my amulet, though."

He holds out the shattered remains of a tree of life amulet, a twin to the one I first summoned when I bonded to the journal. "I couldn't get back until the Shield was weak enough for me to cross."

This is why Elaine was able to contact him: he was in the Otherworld, but not as a spirit.

He's alive.

Fin's snarl cuts through my rising elation. "You boys just don't know when to die."

A wicked grin spreads across Liam's lips. "You're one to talk, you sack of rotted flesh. You can barely hold yourself together, can't you? Let's see what you can do in a fair fight."

Liam shoots forward. I move after him and together we confront Fin. My brother has always been my sparring partner, never my teammate, but in that moment our teamwork is flawless. When Liam attacks, I defend, and when Fin blocks my blows, Liam takes the opening to land his own.

We drive Fin back, landing punches and slashes. The Shield cracks again, and I drive my knife into Fin's leg, deep enough to reach bone. He howls, his fist striking out and catching the side of my face with bony knuckles. I stumble, but Liam holds me upright.

Fin's once-regal clothing is nearly in tatters. I can see his entire body working where bits of muscle show through torn and bloodied skin.

Then suddenly we're awash with light.

Gran, Nora, Elaine, and Roy have arrived. They must have defeated the wraiths in the ballroom and gotten the guests to safety, though some have come with them that I recognize: Dilara, Alice, and the Andrades. They thrust their magic into the splintering Shield. The black cracks recede, the light growing brighter.

Fin wheezes, struggling to stay standing. The color drains from what little bits of his skin are still fully intact and he sways, dropping to one knee.

"It's over," I tell him. "Return to the Otherworld and take your wraiths with you."

Fin laughs, a loud wheezing sound. "I'll never go back there. I will bring my people home."

Something about the way he says it pulls at me. Fin and his people were driven out of Ireland. They were forced away from their home into a place that they hated, and everything he's done since has been to get them back.

To get them home.

But it's too late now. The people crossing the veil aren't who they were when they entered it. Their bodies have long since faded, magic all that sustains them now, and their minds and spirits have turned dark.

Still, I understand.

"You don't have to do this," I tell him. "What happened to you and your people was wrong, but this isn't the answer. You've hurt so many people, and destroying the Shield is only going to hurt more."

Every word I speak is hard. This is the man who killed my parents—all I want is revenge for the pain he's caused me.

But I see now what revenge has done to him, what it will do to me if I don't let it go: it eats away at you, until there's nothing left of who you are.

With great effort, I force myself to lower my blades. "You have to move on, Fin," I say. "You have to let go."

As I say it, I feel the knot of emotions inside me releasing, because it's not just him I'm giving permission to, but myself. Somewhere inside those feelings, I seize hold of the cord that binds us, and through it I can feel his anguish and pain and anger, and he can feel mine.

He holds my gaze, and I hear his voice in my mind, more feeling than words. *I am scared of what comes next.*

So am I. But you are not alone.

I look to the shapes in the Shield, to the people who have followed him across realms and centuries, and his head turns with mine.

Something new breaks through the link. Something warm and peaceful.

Something like understanding.

Bit by little bit, flecks of golden light rise from the King of the Dead's body. He starts to glow, as do those across the Shield. Like snow caught by a whirlwind, the light peels away, funneling toward the Shield in an arc.

The Shield burns brighter and brighter, until the last of Fin's body and those of his people disperse into light with a brilliant flash. Then the light fades, and I watch as the Shield slowly disappears.

The only sounds are Anna's quiet sobs. She sits huddled on the ground, her body wrapped around Max's, shaking.

CHAPTER 31

Colin

My heart is on fire. There's no other way I can explain the pain exploding through my body, the way my chest feels like someone's driving a corkscrew through it, or why breathing feels impossible.

I drop beside Anna and throw my arms around her. There's nothing I can say, so I just sit there and hold her, tears tracking down my cheeks.

I want so badly to keep it all in. To make the pain stop, but I know now that I can't do that. Life isn't all joy and flight; it's also raw aches and pains. It's loving someone so much it makes it hard to breathe, and then letting them go.

It's good and it's bad and it's too much to keep contained inside you.

So I don't stop the tears. I don't hold back. I just hold Anna while the world moves around us.

A soft chill tickles my wrist.

When I open my eyes, Max's spirit stares up at me. I nearly

choke. Anna hiccups. For a moment we all simply stare, and then Max sits back on his haunches, draws a front leg against his stomach, and performs a theatric bow.

A smile cracks across Anna's face. "If you weren't dead right now, I'd bop you," she says thickly, her eyes red and raw from crying.

Max's eyes sparkle mischievously, and my heart wrings.

"No." I shake my head. "This can't be the end. I won't let it be."

My fingers dig into the dark fur of Max's body, my hands trembling. Every restraint I ever wrapped around myself is gone, and my grief is bare.

Max shakes his head sadly as Anna says, "There's nothing you can do, Colin."

But I don't listen. I pull his body from Anna, wrapping him in my arms. Tears run down my cheeks, and I hold him close.

"I don't believe that," I say, thinking of what Fin said to me. *You inherited a sliver of my power.*

A power that could absorb life, and maybe, just maybe, give it back.

I delve deep into the magic inside me, and then I reach out, seeking Max's energy. Jabberwockies were born of the Shield, their bodies as much made of spirit as blood and bone. Just like Max gave us his energy, maybe I can return it.

I pull the energy free of the Shield, drawing it out like a rope, just as Fin did to me.

Max's spirit straightens—then his entire form begins to glow. The faded Shield comes alight once more, brilliant in its luminance. Max's edges blur, his form turning to pure light and condensing into a small ball. It sinks into his body.

The tiny cat takes a ragged breath and stirs in my arms.

Anna lets out a strangled laugh, throwing her arms around both of us and tackling us to the ground. Max wriggles out of my arms, looking in awe at one paw and then the other. Then Anna's whole family is there, patting him on the head and scratching behind his ears.

It worked. It really worked.

"How is that possible?" Anna asks as I scoop him up and we stand.

"Fin said that I inherited some of his power," I say. "I thought since he could absorb energy, maybe he could return it too. That maybe I could . . ." I trail off, staring down at my hands.

"I can't believe I did that," I mutter.

What does it mean that I inherited the power of the King of the Dead? What does that make me?

"Oh, this is going to be fun to explore," Elaine says, running her hands together. "We should start researching."

Roy rolls his eyes. "Is there anything you can't make boring?"

She flicks his shoulder, and he wraps her in a hug.

"Colin." Liam's voice hits me, another relief. I still can't believe he's okay, that he made it back. He nudges my shoulder to look at something behind me, and I turn.

Illuminated in the fading Shield light are two spirits, their faces set with matching smiles. Our parents look happy, their hands laced together.

Peaceful.

"Bridget, Niall." Roy starts toward them, then stops, hesitating. Elaine and Nora flank him, each seemingly unable to find the words they want.

It's my mom who speaks. "What's past is past," she says. "We learned that too late."

"Thank you for taking care of our son," Dad says. "We should have trusted you to from the beginning."

Tears track down Roy's face, and his sisters each take one of his arms. "We'll never stop," Roy assures them. "Both of them are safe with us."

"Do you have to go?" I ask, my voice breaking. I expect to want to hold my breath, to hold everything inside, but I don't. My eyes are filled with tears, but I don't even wipe them away.

Mom smiles warmly. "Haven't you learned anything from your time here?" she teases. "What's dead needs to stay dead."

Then she looks pointedly at Max. "Cheater."

Max sticks out his tongue.

Liam bumps me with a shoulder. Tears race down his cheeks, too, but he smiles. "Come on. Death is only temporary. We'll see them again."

Somehow, that actually makes me feel better, and that's how I know I'm exactly where I belong.

Dad drops down to pat Max on the head. "You take good care of our boys, Maxwell," he says, and Max gives him a one-paw salute.

Mom locks eyes with us. "We love you."

I smile. "We love you too."

Then all together, we watch them walk into the fading mist.

CHAPTER 32

Anna

We sell the guests on the usual special-effects story, claiming we'd been reenacting the origins of Samhain with a light show and mock battle. Some of them look more skeptical than others, but most had fled out front when all the chaos was happening, where the house would have blocked their view of the battle. Besides, with the Shield hidden once more and no evidence of Fin's body, there isn't much for them to challenge us on.

Once they've been seen to, we all collapse into our beds. The house put an extra one in Colin's room so he and Liam wouldn't be separated, and last I saw, Max was curled up on Colin's pillow.

It's late afternoon by the time I rise, tromping into the kitchen to the scent of brewing coffee and the chatter of my family. Everyone else is already awake, and I slide into a chair at the table beside Colin, who's showing Liam the knife marks from his training.

I barely get a glass of orange juice before Nora's doling out tasks. We spend the rest of the morning and early afternoon cleaning up the inn. A lot of the decorations will have to be replaced, which I know bothers Nora to no end. She spent a very long time collecting everything.

Most of my family sustained minor wounds last night, but nothing serious. Gran splinted Colin's wrist and I have a few bruises from Fin's telekinesis, but for the most part the house is the only one with any serious damage. Most of it the house can repair on its own, but Uncle Roy still has to take his truck down to the local hardware store for some wood and paint.

Liam regales us with tales from the Otherworld while we work, and we tell him about what happened with Fin and Kaden on our side, and all the while I wait for him to ask Colin the question that I don't want to hear.

Now that Liam's here, Colin doesn't need us anymore.

By the time we have the place in decent shape that evening, we're all exhausted. The twins disappeared over an hour ago, no doubt to crawl into their beds and sleep some more. Gran is nowhere to be found, and Aunt Elaine and Uncle Roy are on the porch drinking tea. Nora, ever the diligent one, is packaging the leftover food with Liam's help.

"Just a small break." I drag Colin over to the remnants of the bonfire and drop into a seat.

He lowers himself slowly down beside me. Though he tries to hide it, his stiffness is obvious. He went blow for blow with an ancient king and still helped clean up; I'm not complaining.

Max joins us, curling up in Colin's lap.

"I heard Nora say she's going to start working with you on your powers," he says. "You're going to do a reading?"

I grin, propping my feet up on the fire pit edge, and grab us each a still cold root beer from the cooler. "Soon! Apparently psychometrists can also read the history of objects. I can help people find lost things like a pocket dragon or tell them stories about people and things they don't know from their past."

"That's awesome," he says. "Anna the anecdotalist."

"You made that one up."

"An anecdotalist is someone who is skilled at telling stories or—"

I groan, and Colin laughs. I nudge his shoulder. "What about you? Now that Liam's back . . ." I trail off, but Colin gets where I was going.

"I guess we'll go back to traveling around." He stares down at his root beer. "I know he's anxious to start hunting again."

My heart jerks, and I try for a reassuring smile, but it crumbles. I don't want him to leave. But Liam's his family, and family sticks together. I won't come between that.

"You'll be able to help him now," I say, trying to focus on the positive. "He can teach you even more about your powers."

He nods, but he doesn't seem as excited as I expect him to. In fact, he looks a lot like the boy he was when he first showed up at Ravenfall: lost, with the world spinning out of control around him.

He tries for a smile, and it's almost as bad as mine. "I had this idea, where I could start a new journal for myself, and you could do all the drawings, and it'd be both of ours."

My throat tightens. "Well, this way, you both get to keep your parents' journal with you."

Colin plays with the trinity knot around his neck at the mention of his parents. "What do you think Liam meant, death is only temporary?"

I sip my drink. "Do you believe in an afterlife?"

"I think so." His hand closes around the charm. "I'm just not sure about in what form."

"I don't really think the form matters," I reply, tipping my bottle at Max. "I mean, Max would say it's a black cat."

Max cracks open one eye. A smile creeps across Colin's lips.

"And Aunt Elaine would tell you it's a giant library," I continue. "All I know is this life isn't the only one, and for as much as we know, there are still powers at work that we can never understand. And as far as I'm concerned, they can stay that way."

Colin smirks. "Of course. Because where's the fun in knowing everything?"

I grin. "See? You're learning."

"It's been known to happen," he says, sipping his drink.

I lower my feet to the ground. "I have something for you."

I pull a thin wrapped present out of my pocket and hand it to him. For a moment he simply looks at it, and I worry I've made him feel awkward by giving him something. Is it too much? Do friends do this stuff for each other?

Finally, he says, "No one outside my family has ever given me a present before."

I stiffen, already kicking myself for doing this wrong yet again. Panicking, I reach for the present, but he pulls it away, a smile building on his face.

"I didn't mean it that way," he says. "What I meant was, thank you."

The tension floods out of me, and I slump in my seat.

Colin is methodical about the way he unwraps the present. It takes everything I have to sit there and let him peel free each piece of tape with careful precision, and by the time he's done, the wrapping looks like it's never been used.

He unfolds the paper inside, and his entire body goes rigid.

I drew his parents sitting on the porch swing with him and Liam, smiles on their faces. Max perches on Colin's shoulders, and the Charger sits in the background with a setting sun.

"You said you didn't even have a photo of them, so I thought you might want one," I say.

When Colin doesn't move, I nearly groan. This was a bad idea. He lost his parents and just had to say goodbye to them, and here I've gone and shoved a giant reminder of their deaths straight into his hands.

"This is amazing." The words are more breath than sound. I relax, and he looks at me, his bright gray eyes as alive as I've ever seen them. "Thanks, Anna. Really."

I smile, toying nervously with one curl of my hair. "You're welcome," I say. "Anything for a friend."

And before I can say anything, he throws his arms around me in a hug.

I try not to let it feel like goodbye.

CHAPTER 33

Colin

Anna and I sit by the fire pit for a while, watching the leaves flutter to the ground and sipping our drinks. My first night at Ravenfall feels so far away now, though it's only been a couple weeks.

Everything inside me feels still for the first time in days. My parents are dead, but they aren't gone, not really. I can feel them with me, and I have Anna's drawing to keep them close.

I'm not alone.

Footsteps rustle through the grass and I look up to see Liam coming toward us. He's got my bag in his hand. "Are you ready to head out?" he asks. "I want to hit the road before it gets dark."

My stomach turns. I knew this was coming, and it's what I want: me and Liam together again. But I hadn't realized he meant to leave so quickly.

I glance at Anna, but she only stares at a spot on her shoe that couldn't be less interesting. But I know her well enough now to tell when she's trying not to be upset. I know because I feel the same way.

"Yeah, okay," I say, setting my half-empty root beer aside. Max's green eyes narrow in displeasure as I slide him off my lap.

"Do you want to say goodbye to everyone?" Liam asks, already checking his watch.

Anna finally looks up at me, and I see my own thoughts reflected in hers: this isn't goodbye. There's no way after everything we've been through that this is the end.

"How about I'll see you later instead?" she asks, and Max bobs his head in agreement.

I smile. "Definitely. Will you tell everyone else? I don't know . . . I can't say goodbye any more today."

"Of course."

I follow Liam to the front of the house where the Charger idles, waiting for us. We slide in just like old times, him in the driver's seat, me beside him, the windows down and the engine humming. He tosses my bag in the back seat.

"We're heading toward Seattle," he says. "I got a tip about a vampire nearby who's been hunting locals."

The idea of going on a hunt with my brother should excite me. This is what I wanted. So why do I feel so empty?

"Colin?"

Liam watches me carefully, a knowing look in his eye. "Tell me what you're thinking."

Not long ago, I would have told him it was nothing. That I was fine. I'd have bottled it up and dealt with it myself, determined not to be a burden.

This time, I tell him the truth.

"I don't want to move anymore," I say. "I want a place I can call home. I want . . . I want to stay at Ravenfall."

I expect Liam to be upset, to tell me that's not an option. So when a smile takes over his whole face, making his eyes crinkle at the edge, I just stare at him.

"I thought you might," he says. "I didn't want to bring it up in case you felt as if I was pressuring you to stay, but Nora already said it's okay. She took your room off the booking list and everything."

My heart leaps. "She did?"

He nods, and then I'm in his arms and he's holding me tight, and it feels so good to have him back. I know I'd trade all the magic in the world not to have to let him go.

"You could probably stay too," I tell him when I finally pull away. "Wick needs Ravens."

"So does the rest of the world," he replies grimly. "Now more than ever. Besides, I've never been like you when it comes to staying put. Moving every few weeks was more my style, and there's a lot of people out there who can use my help. But I'll stay if you want me to."

I almost say yes. I just got him back, and we've both lost so much the last few weeks. But I've gained just as much, and I know that this isn't really goodbye.

"It's okay," I say. "*I'm* okay."

He ruffles my hair, a habit I had *not* missed, and grabs my bag from the back seat. "I'll come back to check on you all the time, and I put a new phone in your bag. Call me whenever you need me."

I take the bag, clutching it to my chest as I climb out of the car. "I will."

Liam smiles at me through the passenger window, his bangs falling across his brow. "I'm really proud of you, Colin. You're going to be a great Raven."

The words fill me up, and I wonder how I could have ever thought smothering my emotions made me stronger.

Right now, I'm unstoppable.

"Wait!" I say as Liam shifts the car into drive. I fish the journal out of my bag. "You should take this. You'll need it more than me if you're out hunting. I can start a new one."

Liam considers the journal. "Why don't you keep it for now? I'll be able to pull from it wherever I am, and you can use it as a model for yours. I'll come for it in a couple weeks."

I retract my hand. "Is that a promise?"

He smirks. "It's a promise."

I'm still grinning when the car disappears down the driveway.

I take a quick detour inside to toss my bag down a laundry chute—the house grumbling a hello—and then I'm through the kitchen and out onto the porch.

Anna is still sitting at the bonfire, drawing shapes in the dirt with the toe of her shoe while Max pats her comfortingly with a paw.

I jog down the grassy hill and she looks up, hopeful.

"I'm staying." I drop onto the bench beside her. "For as long as you'll let me."

She laughs, throwing her arms about my neck, and Max leaps up onto my shoulders to headbutt me.

"How does forever sound?"

I grin. "Out of this world."

The sun has nearly set now, basking us in gentle light. It feels amazing, and I close my eyes, relishing it.

The fresh autumn scent of the grounds, the familiar creaking of the house settling in, the warmth of Max on my shoulders—they've taken the place of all my old lonely feelings. Tomorrow, I'll take over Anna's chores while she practices her powers with Nora, and later, Elaine will roll out the big table from the kitchen and we'll train in the crisp afternoon air, and at the end of the day, I'll go to sleep in a room that's mine. Really, mine.

Ravenfall is everything my parents had to give up to keep us safe. They loved this place once. The life of it, the magic. Now I'll love it enough for all of us. Because if there's one thing I've learned the last few months, it's that I belong here.

I'm home.

When I open my eyes, Anna is staring at me, a smile plastered across her lips. She holds out her root beer bottle to me. I clank the top of mine against hers, and then the bottom.

"To the long and recently dead," she says.

I grin. "May they stay that way for the days to come."

DON'T MISS THE SPELLBINDING
SEQUEL TO *RAVENFALL* . . .

HOLLOWTHORN

Coming Fall 2023!

ACKNOWLEDGMENTS

This is a book I never thought I'd see published. It's an early story I wrote and set aside years ago when it didn't get me an agent, then revisited after the publication of *The Storm Crow,* only to realize that what I'd thought was a young adult novel was actually a fun, whimsical middle-grade story. So just getting to write acknowledgments for a story I never thought would make it this far is kind of surreal, and so many people helped get it here.

To my agent, Carrie Pestritto: I think this book caught both of us by surprise, but as always, I'm thankful to have you in my corner. This one's journey was certainly an interesting ride.

To my editor, Hannah Hill, whose excitement and support of this book have absolutely blown me away. It means so much to work with someone who's such a fan of the story and the things that inspired it. Thank you for all the *Supernatural* references and for being such an incredible champion of Anna and Colin's (and most importantly, Max's) story, and thank you to the Delacorte team!

As always, I wouldn't have gotten through this journey without my Guillotine Queens: Sam Farkas, Jessica Jones, Brittney Arena, Kat Enright, Jennifer Gruenke, Tracy Badua, Alyssa Colman,

Ashley Northup, and Rae Castor. This group is my rock, and I will forever be thankful for you all.

To Shannon and Joss, my SprintitySprintSprints, thank you for all your Sunday mornings. We'll be back in coffee shops soon, but for now I'll be there in a second, grabbing tea and a bagel!

To Rosiee Thor, for always reading my manuscripts and showing up in my DMs with a "what if you just—" that completely changes and fixes everything, and to Linsey Miller, for our very therapeutic chats.

Thank you to Rowan Witebsky (happy now, Rowan?!) for reading this too many times instead of working on her own writing. You did catch all my logical inconsistences, though, so maybe one day I'll return the favor (*hint, hint*).

Finally, I have the most amazing and supportive group of friends and family, who make this whole process endlessly easier and more enjoyable. Thank you to all of you, and to my mom and dad: I love you.

ABOUT THE AUTHOR

KALYN JOSEPHSON is a fantasy author living in the California Bay Area. She loves books, cats, books with cats, and making up other worlds to live in for a while. She is also the author of the Storm Crow duology.

kalynjosephson.com